COME CLIMB WITH ME

TREES ARE MY BUDS

Revised Edition

By

Jackie Lynn Healey

ISBN

E-book: 9798993481012

Paperback: 9798993481005

Hardcover: 9798993481029

Published by

Planet Earth Publishing, LLC

Foley, AL 36535

Printed in the United States of America

DISCLAIMER

This is a work of fiction. Names, characters, places, and events are either products of the author's imagination or used fictitiously. Any resemblance to actual persons, living or dead, events, or locales is purely coincidental

DEDICATION

To all who believed in me with unwavering faith, who waited patiently, trusting, encouraging, and knowing all along, I had this deep desire to inspire and entertain readers. Thank you, and God bless you.

And to Zacchaeus and Jesus for the Scriptural inspiration that spurred me to see beyond the obvious.

Zacchaeus

Luke 19:4, 5 KJV

4 "And he ran before, and climbed up in a sycamore tree to see him: for he was to pass that way."

5 "And when Jesus came to the place, he looked up, and saw him, and said unto him, Zacchaeus, make haste, and come down, for today I must abide in thy house.

ACKNOWLEDGMENT

I owe the deepest gratitude to a very wonderful young author and friend, McKenna Rowell. McKenna generously provided her time, advice, and guidance, helping me navigate the labyrinth of writing apps, platforms, and services.

I also must praise Janet Jefferson from Author Impact Agency for patiently assisting me in transitioning my manuscript to publication. Thank you for coaxing 'Come Climb with Me' across the finish line.

TABLE OF CONTENTS

Contents

Come Climb With Me: Trees Are My Buds

CHAPTER 1
Baker Park

Saturday Morning

"Get up, Timothy. Breakfast is almost ready," Mom bellows from the kitchen downstairs.

It's unbelievable. I'm twelve years old, going on thirteen. Why doesn't she call me Tim, or Allen, my middle name? Both names are cooler than Timothy.

"I'll be down in five minutes, Mom." I quickly rub my eyes, splash cold water on my face, run a comb through my hair and throw on my oldest pair of jeans, a loose, comfortable T-shirt, thick socks and my hiking boots.

Nobody sleeps late at our house. It's a waste of time. There are things to do. We all share household chores. Dad and I share the outside duties, and I help Mom by emptying trash bins and waste baskets, making my bed, keeping clutter picked up and put away, knocking out my homework promptly and doing whatever is asked of me.

Saturdays are typically my 'All Mine' day. No chores to do, if I'm lucky, or hassles, like having to tag along to a wedding for people I don't even know. I can hang out on Saturdays, make my own plans and just have fun.

We live in Highlands, a small town in New Hampshire. We have one movie complex, 4-5 grocery stores, about 7-8 churches, two elementary/middle schools and one huge, sprawling high school. Highlands has everything we need and not too much extra of anything. And it's a very kid-friendly town. We can ride our bikes and get to the farthest streets in 30 minutes or less.

I'm heading to the park behind the middle school after breakfast. Baker Park has our neighborhood's oldest, biggest, and best trees. But long before I discovered the magic of trees, I went there for the slides, monkey bars, teeter-totters, merry-go-rounds and sand.

But now? Now I'm older. There's no more juvenile playground hoopla. I've upped my game to the major leagues - tree-climbing. Extreme risk. Drama. Adventure.

Baker Park is still the venue, but now I delve far beyond the kiddy section. The vast, treed expanse tucked in the back of the park gives me the solitude I need to hide, think, and dream – the important teenage stuff. Plus, I get to test my agility, push boundaries, discover, and face fear, danger, and the unknown. And I get to wow myself with my mastery of navigating death-defying heights, expansive, perilous empty spaces, and dangling from precariously slender, weak branches.

But, hey! In case you didn't know, it's personal, too. Trees are my friends. They never argue or fight. I can be myself. And they're always glad to see me.

***

Mom is in the pantry as I finish breakfast. She is either making a shopping list or planning dinner.

"Can I go to the park?" I ask. Asking is like getting your foot in the door. Why would she object when I'm asking so politely?!

"Sure, Timmy. Just be safe, and don't be gone too long," Mom cautions me.

I'm out of here. I bound out the back door, then leap off the porch, just like I'm the Flash.

I cut across the backyard and race down two blocks to Baker Park. It's still early, and I have the park all to myself.

I run through 20 to 30 trees to get to the farthest back corner. It's so peaceful. This section has no walking paths, ponds, benches, playgrounds or picnic tables. The park is completely void of any human presence. It's just me and all these beautiful, old, tall oak trees. They are my favorite trees. Climbing them is so easy and fun. This stand of oaks is my best find ever.

These tall, old oak trees are lonely. You can just tell by looking at them. They need a true, no-hassle best friend in the worst way. And I'm their guy! I bet nobody has ever climbed these trees. That's crazy because most are probably over 200 years old. That's almost back to the beginning of time.

Ugh! I know; not really.

But I could be the first human to stand before this hidden gem of nature, especially if you imagine they grew from acorns, with no human intervention, right where they fell.

Then I snap back into reality.

Wait. Listen. Do you hear that? I have company.

Squirrels are everywhere - on the ground, tree trunks and branches. I'm sure they think I'm in *their* yard and on *their* turf. And the birds are aware of my presence, too. They gawk at me with cautious eyes, flicking their heads all about. They switch branches and flutter off to safer trees, tweeting and chirping out warnings as they resettle and continue their wary watch.

Like most kids, I talk to myself. We might be alone, but we think, and even speak, as though we're conversing with someone or something we've personalized. It fulfills that inner need for companionship. 'Mr. Green' is one of my Baker Park tree 'friends.' You must go to that mystical world to walk in that reality. It's natural for us kids.

"How are you today, Mr. Green?" I ask. My buds, the trees, don't have real names, but they always welcome me and pay attention to everything I say.

Right, Tim. I bet they do. Ha!

Mr. Green always has the same taunting reply, "Hey, boy. I've been waiting for you. Are you sure you're ready for me?"

As I clear the eight feet of trunk, I slowly climb vertically from limb to limb. I stay close to the main shoot, where every limb is strong and sturdy. I like to climb at least halfway up before I inch horizontally across the outstretched branches. That's where I find the most secluded and peaceful spots. I can lean or stretch out, lie flat, or hunker down, camouflaged by the trunk and foliage like a hunter, lookout, or spy.

At this point, I am 25 feet off the ground when I see a cool fork in a limb that I know is beckoning me to come and stretch out. That's when the feeling of tranquility usually starts to settle in. I can plan and daydream. I can lie on my back and let my eyes explore nature's hidden wonders - owl dens, squirrel and bird nests, beehives. Or, even better, I can spend all day watching the clouds slowly glide past, unaware that I'm watching them.

Suddenly, I notice something strange and out of place.

Someone fastened a rope to the branch six feet from where I sit. Somebody has been here before me!

My heart races, and my mind soars as I lie down on my belly and slither further out the limb to check out this unexpected mystery.

The rope is incredibly old and rotten. The rain, wind, cold, heat, and time have bleached the color out and worn its fibers down. I'm sure birds and squirrels pecked and gnawed it, too. But the rope is still looped around the branch and is holding something in place. Most people would bury things. I would never have thought of doing this.

I crawl along the branch beyond the security of the fork and lie spread out, still on my belly, to get within reach. As I fiddle with the rope, it almost disintegrates between my fingers as I untie the knot. Once it is untied, I unwind the rope from around the branch. I immediately discover the rope is holding what looks like a sardine can in place on the underside of the branch. That's a sure sign there's something valuable inside.

Jackpot! It's going to be money, or the key to a treasure chest and map. What else could it be?

I'll bet someone hid it here at least ten years ago. Somebody probably robbed a store, and the police were hunting for them. This was a perfect hiding spot. It could have happened that way! The who and why questions kept pinging around in my head like a pinball in an old-fashioned arcade game.

Duct tape encircled the sardine can so that water wouldn't get inside. Or squirrels! I use a twig from a nearby branch to saw through the tape. Somebody wanted this to not only stay in place but to remain secure and hidden.

"Hello, Mr. Green. Any idea how long this has been here?" I knew he wouldn't answer, but in my world, I have conversations with trees and animals all the time. And they answer me, sometimes at least, in my imagination. Mr. Green said it has been there a long time. "Thanks, Captain Obvious!" I quipped.

I grab the can and rope and retreat to my original resting spot at the fork in the branch. I dangle my feet through the limbs and sit on the confluence of the two branches. Lifting the lid, I discover a folded paper concealing something flat and firm. Eureka! I'm guessing it's a rare gold coin! A doubloon or two, maybe?

Just as I had hoped and expected. It's a hidden treasure! And it's very old.

"Tim, old boy! You've struck it rich!" I said to myself. And I bet the paper will lead you to the bigger prize, the pirate chest filled with gold, silver, jewels, rings, bracelets, brooches, chains with huge, heavy medallions, hundreds of coins, goblets and fancy inlaid daggers!! (Screenwriters can't even make up stories this cool!)

The coin is silver, not gold. It's worn, and its images are unclear. One side shows a large, old-world-style cross, a castle, and a small bird. A bust is on the opposite side, with an inscription at the top. The date below the bust is hard to read, but it looks like it says 1678. That makes it almost three hundred fifty years old! Spanish explorers or conquistadors may have brought it to the Americas. More than likely, they didn't, but it's okay to imagine.

Someone folded the paper five or six times to fit it in the can. The ink leaked through the folded edges, making the message nearly impossible to read.

Better light will help, I surmise, so I refold it and stuff it and the coin in my back pocket. I'll take it all home and figure everything out there. A Google search for the coin should be easy. It's probably valuable, and I'll be rich AND famous! I dropped the sardine can and rope to the ground; I'll take them home, too.

Climbing down was no sweat. I was only up twenty-five feet at the highest point; it's less than ten feet from the lowest branch to the ground. I drop straight and land on my feet, right beside the can and rope, so I bend down and pick them up.

Like a gazelle escaping from a pride of lions, I sprint through the trees and out of the park. Despite being alone, I remain vigilant, checking all around and behind for muggers or witnesses. But what's the crime? It's playground rules out here. Finders-keepers. Right?

This is so cool. I have never discovered anything valuable or mysterious, ever. And up in a tree, of all the crazy places to hide something. Who will believe this? Who would do something like this? And why?

I was huffing as I reached our backyard. I vaulted up and over the two back porch steps, landing hard. I yanked the door open, quickly bulldozing through the gap like a 200-pound linebacker.

"Hey, Mom. I'm back. I'm heading up to my room," I announce, navigating through the kitchen and living room furniture before taking the stairs two steps at a time to reach my bedroom.

I'll keep this quiet for now. I need to solve these mysteries before discussing them. Entering my room, I ease the door shut, put the can, rope, coin, and paper on the desk, and turn on my study lamp.

'What have we got here, my mateys? Come closer. Let's see,' I said in my best pirate impression.

CHAPTER 2
Mysteries

Late Saturday Afternoon

I untie my boot laces and pry them off, pushing each with my toe against the opposite heel. They lay right where they fall. My goal is to get comfortable. Which I accomplish. Now I can get to work.

Thank goodness for 5G internet. I hit the power button and my laptop boots up in less than 15 seconds. I never time it. It's just fast - like lightning!

"Hi, Google. I need your help." I always verbalize my thoughts when I'm alone. I promise, it's not crazy. It's my personal, private world. I can do whatever I want.

I'm so anxious and excited. I hope the search is quick and the results are all positive. I've held a few old coins before, but I never owned one. Can I even say this one is mine now? What if someone hid it just for safekeeping and wants it back? Should I even try to find 'him'?

My Google search for old Spanish coins was easy. But finding the precise coin was a bit more challenging. That piece of the puzzle took forever - at least an extra five or six minutes.

I had to compare photos with my coin, back and forth, over and over.

It turns out 'my coin' is a Colonial Era Bolivian silver Spanish 1-Real (ree-Al) Charles II, minted in 1678. I found it on an Internet coin seller's website. The shop wants $210 for theirs.

Boy! That would be a nice wad of dough in my pocket.

I could get a metal detector or a drone with several spare batteries, a charger AND a carrying case for that much money. I would probably even have cash left over. Would I sell it? It's something to think about.

I print out the page with the picture of the comparable coin so I will have a permanent record of the coin's description and value. Now, when I tell my parents and friends about it, they won't have to take my word for it. Smart thinking, Tim!

Next, I move on to the ink-splotched paper. It looks more like a tie-dyed T-shirt than a note. The tape around the sardine can didn't seal it very well. A bit of moisture penetrated the taped lid, probably many times over the years, causing the ink to bleed through the multiple folds and layers of paper.

I carefully unfold it once again and use the palms of my hands to smooth out the creases. I don't want it to tear, but I need it completely flat to figure out what's written. I flip it over so I can smooth it out from both sides. It's slow work, but my patience finally pays off. I did it! And with no adult guidance or supervision.

Deciphering the original message is difficult. It proceeds slowly; one word, then sometimes just one letter at a time. I use a magnifying glass to decipher the worst smudges. "You're so good at this, Tim. Kudos, bud!" I hype myself at every little win.

I transcribe everything onto a separate, blank sheet of paper. It takes an hour, maybe an hour and a half, to decipher it accurately and completely. My initial reaction, I hate to admit, is more dejection than elation. It's just a personal time capsule. No map. No more hidden treasure. Just a dead-end note. I feel so deflated.

Like the note, my fantasy just got waterlogged. Oh, well!

The message read:

Hi!

I'm Johnny Butler. I'm 18. The Army sent me a draft notice, and I leave for boot camp next month. My parents are worried, but I'm sure I'll be fine.

I just wanted to leave something behind for a mystery friend who loves to climb trees, just like me. And you're climbing in my favorite tree, no less!

This old Spanish coin is a keepsake given to me by my middle school history teacher. He knew I loved his class and everything about history. (I guess it pays to be a curious, courteous, kind, obedient student. I'm not sure I was, but I tried to be.)

Anyway. Here it is - a secret treasure squirreled away in my favorite go-to place.

I'm sure your imagination goes wild when you're climbing. I know, as a former and fellow tree-climber, that's one reason I climbed - to be alone, think and imagine.

So, I wonder where this coin will take YOU as you think about its long history. To Spain? Aboard a pirate ship? Did it fall out of a merchant's coin purse? Was it part of somebody's ransom payment? I'm still stoked about the many places my imagination took me every time I turned this coin over in my hand!

Your friends will probably go bonkers, and they'll be envious if they're anything like my friends.

Congratulations!

Enjoy it, my friend.

Happy climbing. And be safe.

Your friend,

Johnny, 1968.

***

"Supper time, Tim," Mom called from the foot of the stairs. She might have been curious, but she left me alone whenever I went up to my bedroom and closed the door. She will ask me how my day went and what I did all day during supper. That's not so unpredictable. It's our dinner routine.

I stuff the coin, Johnny's note, and my paper with the deciphered text in my back pocket. I hurry downstairs to the kitchen and breakfast nook, where we eat all of our meals (unless we have company).

"Wash your hands, bud!" Mom was fanatical about that. I don't know if I'd call her a Clean Freak, but I never think that much about washing my hands. But never question or try to con her. Momma bears are ferocious when you rile them.

"What's for dinner, Mom? It smells great," I exclaimed, taking in a deep breath.

I arrived downstairs in time to help set out the dinner plates and silverware. Mom brought the paper towel roll over and sat it on the table. We only put real napkins out when guests come over for dinner.

"We're having meatloaf, mashed potatoes and green beans, hon," Mom replies. This is a favorite staple in our house. We have it at least once a month, which is fine with me. I'll probably get a meatloaf sandwich or two from the leftovers, with extra ketchup! That's meatloaf icing, man! Heaven on bread!

Dad pulls into the driveway just as Mom is taking the meatloaf out of the oven. He worked all day at the hardware store. This is the week he had to work six days straight. He comes through the back door, greets us all, hugs Mom, and washes his hands at the kitchen sink. As he sits down, he says, "Let's eat. I'm starving!"

"Tim? Will you ask the blessing for us tonight?" Mom or Dad usually asked the blessing, but my prayer is the best because it's always short, quick and to the point.

"Thank you, Lord, for this food we are about to eat. Bless Dad for providing for our needs and Mom for preparing the meal. In Jesus' name, Amen."

I moved on from the prayer we all learned in Sunday School: 'God is great. God is good. Let us thank Him for this food...' There isn't anything wrong with it. I just feel more grown up speaking from what is really on my heart right then. I know it's always the thoughts and our sincerity that matter. I say just be yourself.

Most table conversation is small talk covering typical grown-up things - the daily grind, routines, friends and relatives, life and world events, news around town, etcetera.

As their topics of conversation dwindle, the focus always shifts to me and my day. I'm a carefree soul, and my day always piques their interest. You could say my day is the icing on their I'd-love-to-be-young-again cake.

"Hey, bud, did you get into any fights today? What have you been up to?" Dad asks.

I'm an only child. I grew up in my own sheltered world, entertaining myself a lot. But I'm growing out of it.

Dad knew I was unlikely to find or cause any trouble. It was his bit of gleeful ribbing. But it opens the door for me to join in the table talk.

"I went to Baker Park this morning, climbed a few trees and chilled, mostly. Then, I stumbled upon something so amazing in an enormous oak tree in the back of the park. I couldn't believe it."

When I get excited, I fall into that 'just the facts' mode, and I spill the whole 'can of beans' all at once. It was all out of my mouth in 30 seconds! As I told them my short story, I pulled the note and coin from my back pocket and handed them to Dad. I gave Mom my transcription of Johnny's note.

The old, worn silver coin mesmerized Mom and Dad. Neither of them had ever held a Spanish coin, let alone one so old. They were amazed that I knew what it was and how much it was worth. I had even deciphered the message from the stained and smudged note Johnny left.

Dad looked them over and, in a quick minute, said, "This is neat, Tim. I've never seen or held an old Spanish coin before. Now I know what got you so excited."

"Son, this note is over half a century old. Can you imagine that? He wrote his note before your mom and I were even born." That detail eluded me but was yet another fascinating piece of the adventure.

"I wonder if Johnny Butler is still alive," Mom commented. "Do you think he might still live around here? He would be so excited to know his little time capsule was found and opened."

Mom was so excited and kept adding more to the mystery as we all pondered her questions and observations. And it was clear her mind was racing ninety miles an hour.

"Do you want to know more? If so, I could help you check the newspaper archives and public records," Mom suggested. "Johnny Butler should be in public records. He would be over 70 years old now, though," she added. "That's older than your grandparents, Timmy."

Ugh! TMI! Too Much Information, Mom. I thought what I had found was a big discovery, but the mystery is obviously bigger than I thought and it's still growing.

"It would be cool to meet Johnny, Mom. But going through files and records sounds boring, and just like homework. And I already have plenty of that every day." I wanted to sound excited, but felt ready to move on to my next adventure.

"Can you let me sleep on it, Mom? Is that okay?" I sure didn't want to bust her bubble or spoil the mood.

"Certainly, hon, I need to replay all of this in my head, too," she replies. "Let's talk about it some more tomorrow."

CHAPTER 3
Treetop Gang

Sunday

Sunday mornings are a set-in-stone tradition at our house - breakfast at 8 o'clock, get dressed, Sunday School, then the church service. And then, wait for it, another Sunday tradition. We go to the Piccadilly cafeteria in the mall for a fancy lunch. Many of the church crowd congregate there, even the pastor and his family. Kids from my class are also there with their families, so we always use that opportunity to make plans for after we get changed (out of our church clothes). Following lunch, what's left of the day is usually ours.

"Hey, Mom. Is it okay if some guys from my Sunday School class come over this afternoon?" I ask. "They want to see the coin and Johnny's note," I explain.

I had told everyone in my Sunday School class about the tree-climbing discovery, the old Spanish coin, and the note Johnny Butler had left in the tree over 50 years ago. All the kids were excited and wanted to come over and see the coin and note, climb the tree, and relive the adventure. I suddenly felt a little famous, or at least popular.

"Absolutely, hon," Mom replies. "Just put your church clothes away and make sure your room is straight before they get here," she adds.

"You're the best, Mom. We'll be outside. They want to go over to Baker Park and climb the old oak tree with me."

Once I changed, Dad asked me to help him in the garage. When we got there, he told me to help lift the mower onto his workbench. He brought a new set of blades for it home from the hardware store. He wanted my help to get it off the ground so it would be easier to work on. Once it was on its side on the bench, I held the mower steady for him while he loosened the nut, switched blades, and tightened the nut back snugly. Afterward, we lifted it back onto the garage floor. He started it to make sure the blades were in balance, then he shut it off.

Mission accomplished!

***

Ted, Tommy, and Sam showed up at about 2 o'clock. My folks said hi to them, and then my friends followed me to my room. They sat on the edge of my bed, and I got out Johnny's note and the coin. They passed them around, turned them over, asked me questions, and then batted around a lot more thoughts among themselves. It wasn't quite pandemonium, but their curiosity was very bewildering to me. They were more mesmerized by Johnny Butler than by the coin.

They are consumed by the mysteries surrounding Johnny Butler, just like Mom. I can't believe it.

"Since he went into the Army, did he go to Vietnam? Was he in combat? Did he get wounded or killed? That would mean he got a Purple Heart medal. What if he's still alive? He was probably a hero. Maybe he's famous. Would he meet with us and tell us more about his life? I want to hear more about the teacher who gave him the coin."

The conversation and speculation ramp up the excitement to a whole new level. Everyone wants to go to the park. That's the natural thing to do since I can't resolve their questions. I suggest we head over there and remind them we can talk and speculate all we want then.

We clamor down the stairs and stampede through the living room, hall, and kitchen, then out the back door like a herd of raging, fear-deranged buffalo. I'm sure my parents thought they'd missed a tornado warning siren.

As we meander down the sidewalk towards Baker Park, everyone is vying for attention by tugging at each other's arms and maneuvering to be face-to-face for undivided attention.

I stop abruptly, without explanation, and so does everyone else. They stare at me to see what's wrong.

I reach into my front pocket and pull out a handful of bubblegum. Not just any bubblegum, mind you. This is Bazooka Bubblegum, the name-brand 'Cadillac' of all bubblegum. It's my favorite. And it always will be.

All the chatter comes screeching to a halt.

Bubblegum is magical to guys. You chew it quickly. The aim is to get it soft as fast as possible. You want to be the first to blow a bubble. You want to see who blows the first bubble and then who blows the biggest one. And next, whose bubble is going to burst onto their face? There's no prize, just bragging rights, or the butt of jokes. It's a quick-draw shootout. Nobody moves. Everyone intently watches each other as they chew. It's a stare-down, too. Break their concentration. And don't bite the inside of your jaw. It usually happens. I know from personal experience.

It was a cool, fun, ten-minute interlude before we continued on to the park. And just for the record, you chew bubblegum throughout the rest of the day. No swallowing or spitting it out. It's a macho guy thing. You can add to it, but you can't pitch it - not until you're alone.

"Hey, Tim. Thanks for the bubblegum," Tommy warbles past his gob of gum. "I never think to bring anything with me. You're the best."

"Next time, let's bring a pocket full of Tootsie Rolls and a couple canteens of Gatorade," Ted adds. "Everything is better with chocolate."

"I think we should all bring something along next time and keep it a surprise," Sam insists.

"Nah," I say. "We keep our heads together. Plan it out. That way, everybody pitches in something different."

We arrived at the old oak tree in less than five minutes. I was glad to be back. But I felt an odd sensation this time. It almost seemed like this old oak tree was now a memorial tree, the Johnny Butler Memorial Tree. Of course, I didn't say it out loud. Was I feeling that mysterious, surreal reverence everybody else was feeling?

I was standing in front of my tree pal, 'Mr. Green,' but I couldn't acknowledge him today. I know enough to make sure I don't talk to trees or animals around my friends. They'd rib me about it for my whole life. (Even though I bet they talk to 'things,' too.)

"Hey, guys. Do you mind if I climb up first so I can lead the way?" It's not that important, but it seemed like it was, so they let me. There wasn't anything particularly special about the tree, either, now that I removed the treasure. But there is something special about climbing trees with your friends. We get to hang out, show off, tell jokes, make up weird or funny stories, and laugh.

Four guys will never fit on one branch. Is that a law of physics? I haven't studied that yet, but it seems logical. And it doesn't mean you can't try. At some point, somebody invariably clings to somebody else's arm, and you're holding on to other branches to maintain your balance. I'd say, at minimum, we're in a precarious situation. But isn't that just another way of spelling F-U-N? It's not like we haven't fallen out of a tree before, at least once in our lives, but we don't want to do it in front of all of our friends.

Then, completely out of the blue, I hear someone say, "I think we should take your mom up on her suggestion to look for Johnny Butler." It was Ted. "My mom might even want to help." Wow! Where has his mind been? Where did that come from?

Tommy chimed in next with, "Maybe we could split up the different places to look so it will go faster."

Then Sam put in his own very pragmatic two cents worth. "Let's ask your mom if she'll meet with all of us and our moms and plan out the research. Then we can have a party in two or three weeks, maybe on Sunday afternoon, to combine and hear what everyone has found. You know -- mystery, surprises, and refreshments. We could even name ourselves 'the Treetop Gang!'"

Geez, Louise! I'm thinking I'm back in the 2nd grade.

Sam's idea of a Treetop Gang was a spur-of-the-moment but well-intentioned outburst. He wanted us to be imaginative and explore new tree-climbing opportunities in various parks, using different trees regularly. Something we could all look forward to once a week. Sometimes, we'd go out to climb trees on Saturday and sometimes on Sunday afternoons. Anybody could join the club. The more, the merrier. We'd keep it informal. And we'd have no rules, except one – the majority rules.

I hadn't thought this would be so exciting, but I can see this keeps the quest alive. There's more excitement and adventure yet to come for everyone, evidently. By silent assent, we've even started an informal tree-climbing club.

But, hey.

We're already good friends and now have a great reason to hang out more often.

I've finally come around to sensing the depth of their curiosity and the merits of their input. "Let's pitch this to my mom when we get back to the house and see if she's interested," I exclaimed.

That was the bugle call for heading out.

Back to the corral, pardners!

CHAPTER 4
Wheels Are Churning

Sunday Afternoon

Mom had chips, cookies, and sodas on the table when we came through the back door. I have no idea how she anticipated our arrival, but that's just another quirky knack she has. We all plopped into chairs, hands and arms flailing, reaching across the table over each other for snacks. Then, I paused, just for an instant. All I could hear was a million 'what-ifs' about Johnny Butler. It was just like all the crazy buzzing around a stirred-up beehive!

I didn't even hear someone say, 'Ready. Set. Go!'

Mom, in all the confusion and boisterous excitement, simply held up her right hand as high as she could, just like a polite little kindergartener, or need I say, an 'I-am-in-charge-here' schoolteacher. It had the effect she wanted. Everyone turned their attention to her and the racket died instantly. She then calmly interjected, "Why don't you let me write all your thoughts and questions down, so we don't lose track of what you'd like to find out?"

Everyone politely inclined their heads, perhaps with a bit of embarrassment. Then, one by one, my friends' hands started creeping up timidly to get my mom's attention, which they already had. I quickly took that opportunity to speak for all four of us.

"Mom, the guys and I were talking at the park about you saying it would be neat if we could find out what happened to Johnny Butler after 1968, where he is now, and how excited he would be to know that I discovered his note and coin 50 years after he hid them in the tree. We had an idea that maybe the guys' moms could help you search the public records, and then we could all have a small 'reveal party' to learn what everyone found. That way, everyone will get to be in on the adventure, fun, and excitement."

"That's a super idea, guys. Let me jot down the likely places where public files might have records of Mr. Butler. Then I can call your mothers and see if they have time and want to help. In the meantime, you can tell your mothers what we've discussed, and I'll talk to them in a day or two. A Sunday afternoon would be a wonderful day for your reveal party, too, because we'll need God's help as we try to uncover the mysteries of what happened to Johnny Butler."

Mom was on a roll now. She grabbed her tablet and pen and exclaimed, "So, while you're all here and wired with curiosity, tell us all again, one at a time, what you'd like to know about Johnny Butler. I'll start with Sam and go around the table. Then I'll come back to each of you if you think of something else. Have we got a plan?"

We all nodded our heads in affirmation. I thought we looked like bobblehead dolls.

It was a perfect plan, and Mom had set it in motion right under our noses. Mom made everything seem easy. She had some heavy-duty teacher juice in her.

"So, let's start by writing what we already know about Mr. Butler from his 1968 note. Okay?" Mom exclaims as she humbly beseeches the kitchen congregates for their response. All heads bob their assent one more time as she picks up the deciphered note, starts reading off specific points, and begins jotting the following details on her notepad:

He's 18 years old in 1968, so he was born in 1950.

His nickname is Johnny; real name John or Jonathan.

He joined the Army, in 1967 or 1968; unclear since note not dated.

No mention of which middle school he attended.

No name for his male history teacher.

"Well, as you can see, there's more we don't know about Mr. Butler than what he actually told us in his note," Mom stated. "The fun is just starting for us now that he has captured our attention. We won't give up until we've shaken every branch of every tree in the forest. Right?"

We all wagged our assent, probably for the hundredth time, but her metaphor flew right over our heads. It was 'right' simply because Mom said it.

"So, Sam. What would you be interested in knowing about Mr. Butler that we haven't learned from his note?"

Sam jumped into the deep water with both feet. It's fun participating when all you do is ask questions. At school, all they ever want are answers!

"I thought everybody wanted to go to college after high school. What made him pick the Army instead? Why wasn't he afraid? Did he have friends joining the Army with him? Was he a paratrooper? Was he a tank gunner? Did he play on any of his high school's sports teams?"

Mom's reply was very encouraging. "Good questions, Sam. I especially liked the last one. Do you know why? We can put school newspapers on our list of records to check. And if we find his high school, the alumni secretary might know where he is or what happened to him. I appreciate your thoughts, Sam."

Boy! Talk about floating on Cloud 9. Sam looked like he'd struck gold. You could almost visualize him strutting around the table like a peacock. And he was just the first stop in Mom's tabletop prospecting. Her reaction set up everyone else to loosen their inhibitions and get creative.

Tommy and Ted acted more like someone had let the air out of their tires. Each was thinking along the same lines as Sam. But they each mustered a few additional queries for the mystery pot.

"Did Johnny have brothers or sisters that climbed with him or other schoolmates?" Ted asked.

"Do you suppose he might have lived close to where we live now?" Tommy wondered.

"He might have liked the Army and stayed in so he could travel and see other countries. Is he still in touch with his Army buddies?" I added.

Mom spent the next hour listening, writing, and giving us feedback and encouragement. She had six pages of notes from four wildly enthused young men. Only Johnny Butler could answer many of the questions she had recorded. But it hinges on whether we can find him, if he's still alive, and if he will meet with us. But need I say it? Hope springs eternal! And we're more psyched than ever now.

"I'm going to take a wild guess that we're just getting started, and you'll come up with more questions over the next few days. Would that be a safe bet?" Mom asked.

"I'd say that's definitely a safe bet, Mom."

"So, guys, are you all worn out or just getting wound up?" Mom asks. "No matter. Let's call it a day. It's late Sunday afternoon, and you have school tomorrow. We can pick up our roundtable fun again soon, maybe in the next few days. Will that work?"

All gestured affirmatively and were pushing their seats back from the table when Mom threw out one more meaty bone for the hungry wolf pack. "How about if you all come over for supper on Tuesday? After we finish eating, I'll update you on where we're at and what's happening next."

Ted and Tommy were both rubbing their hands together in jubilation. Sam was grinning from ear to ear. It was obvious they were all pumped.

"I'm thinking this is going to be a real, big adventure, Mrs. Johnson," Sam interjected. "It's going to be tough to get to sleep after we retell all that's happened today to our parents."

"Well, boys. The mystery has stayed hidden for over 50 years, so a few more days won't matter. Tell yourselves to get a good night's sleep. I promise we'll jump on this and move the search further along for you quicker than you can imagine. Johnny Butler hasn't disappeared forever."

There were gleeful stares between the guys around the table and grins galore. Ted even had his arm around Sam's shoulder.

This Treetop Gang, slash Club, has got some wings now and momma bird is flying high, I thought.

What else does Mom have up her sleeve?!

CHAPTER 5
Grown-up Homework

Monday

Unbeknownst to me, Mom was busy working on her public records research list Sunday night. She rarely has idle thoughts or hands, though. Her wheels are always turning.

By Monday morning, Mom had a research list of 14 types of records. She believes in dissecting down to the nitty-gritty and going Hollywood with her finale -- big and flashy. You go, Mom!

(One mental note from the Peanut Gallery: Cheerleaders, yes. Marching bands, no. Sorry, band members.)

***

"Tim! It's Monday morning. Get a move on. Don't forget to brush your teeth. Breakfast will be on the table in five minutes. And don't forget your book bag."

"I won't forget, Mom. I'm all set. I'll be down in a minute," I asserted from the open bathroom door. The weekend is over. Seriously?! Why can't today be a holiday?

"This is a mighty hearty breakfast, Mom. No joke. Cross my heart. You're the greatest mom ever!"

Mom chuckled as she saw my ear-to-ear grin.

The bus was right on time - 7:45, and so was I. A quick kiss on Mom's cheek and I was out the front door and off the porch running. I was at the curb waiting as the bus rolled to a full stop.

Here we go, boys and girls! Let's wow the judges.

***

After I left, Mom brought out her contacts and public records research list and set them on the table with a hot cup of coffee and her notepad. Usually, it was her time to read the morning newspaper.

You could sense her talking to herself subconsciously. It's time to do some refining and set up a group call, Betty.

Monday is the day to put the pedal to the metal. I could visualize her revving up with endless subliminal queries. Will she be peeling out and laying any rubber on this hot, new adventure?

"So, what do I have here?" Mom asked herself. "So far, all you've got are the basics, Betty. Just the basics."

Mom is so methodical. Besides sharing the contact list and assignments with the other mothers, she would wonder what needed to be done to ensure everyone was thorough and consistent. That leads her to jot down some practical and essential Must-Do's.

Log as much as you can:

Date & time of outreach

Name of contact

Contact number/email address

The resource you're researching (newspaper, VFW, etc.)

Result (or dead end)

Notes/comments

And then she adds a key footnote for the group:

If you find ANYTHING on Mr. Butler, call or text the info to the other mothers that same day. And she amplifies, for emphasis - Your 'find' might facilitate someone else's research, such as address, date, family members' or relatives' names uncovered.

Then, like icing, she flags one more important reminder:

Make sure the boys know what's happening. It's a good dinner table discussion topic. We must all stay engaged.

Here is the contact list she shared:

Boy	Mom	Phone	Research Area
Tim	Betty	(603) 247-9812	Papers, query ads, obits, cemetery records
Ted	Casey	(603) 247-2119	Instagram, Facebook, Google, Voter rolls
Tommy	Bonnie	(603) 247-4645	Historical Society, MVA, VFW, Legion
Sam	Lisa	(603) 247-3599	Public school records, school papers

True to her nature, Mom opted for the quick, simple route to starting the research project. She took and shared pictures of Johnny's deciphered note and coin as background info for each mother. She also took and shared pics of the Contacts List with research areas assigned and the log instructions to keep everyone consistent. A 1:45 P.M. FaceTime call would ensure everyone reviewed the plan simultaneously.

Mom would discuss objectives, deadlines, and follow-up FaceTime calls to address progress, issues, and needs and set a target date for the Reveal Party for 14 days from yesterday (Sunday.) She thought it might be ambitious, but it was realistic. And she knew they could always slip it another week if they needed extra time.

Mom's goal was for them to work independently, complete tasks, and communicate regularly. Everyone hoped each mother would uncover some evidence of Johnny Butler in their research. We would measure success by how thoroughly everyone searched, regardless of their findings.

I could hear her inner prayer voice pleading, 'Please, Lord Jesus. Help us find a lot.' Just as the boys formed their Treetop Gang, Mom felt the mothers must team up and pride themselves in their behind-the-scenes work. She was confident that's what moms do best.

Mom

Monday, 1:45 P.M.

"Hey, ladies. Thanks for making yourselves available on short notice. I hope you received my text earlier today and have looked at the snapshots I attached. Did your boys tell you what Timmy found that has gotten everyone excited? They want to know a lot more about Mr. Butler, and frankly, I do, too. Do you need a better synopsis of what started this and what the boys are thinking? Do you have any questions yet?"

All seemed apprehensive about speaking up, so Mom kept going.

"I'd like to start off by saying I was just the first mother to get involved. It started in my kitchen, and I ramrodded the boys' discussions to channel their excitement and energy. They were so enthused that they wanted you involved, too. And frankly, sharing the research responsibilities is better and will be a significant help." She paused.

"So far, my major challenges have been creating an exhaustive research list and divvying it up among us, so the workload is comparatively equal, and ensure there's a good likelihood we will finish together. If any of your research areas seem intimidating, or you feel unqualified to tackle an area, or you'd just like to trade, it's alright. I just ask that you tell me so I can stay abreast of who's doing what."

"Disappointing our boys is the last thing I want to see come out of this, so I pray we can not only find records for Johnny Butler, but him as well, living in our community."

"I know I've heaped some 'crazy' on your already loaded plates with this, but I think we can pull it off."

"Did your boys tell you I invited them over for dinner tomorrow evening? It's a research kickoff to let the boys know we're going to find Mr. Butler and hopefully get answers to every question they've got about him. I'd love to have you come, eat, and stay as well. I know that might be a hard ask with some of your work schedules and other responsibilities, but I wanted to put the invitation out there."

"I'm planning a simple and easy meal, from prep to clean up - paper plates, plasticware, chicken tenders, fries, ketchup, iced tea or fruit punch, carrot sticks, and celery with Ranch dressing and ice cream cups for dessert."

"After dinner, we'll clear everything, take out the trash, and assemble around the table again for a Johnny Butler update. I'll explain that we've spoken, shared what we know, and divided up research areas so we can all start finding out more about Johnny."

"It's a big deal because we want them to know this is important to us, too, and we will not let them down. The only guarantee we can give is that we're going to try hard and get other people around town to help us as much as they can. The story is going to spread, and with it, there will be public interest. That's my hope, anyway."

"It surpasses a simple find; it's far more significant than a fifty-year-old note, an old Spanish coin, a sardine can, and an oak tree in Baker Park. For these boys, it's like we're working on a space mission to Mars. This is their very own, real-life adventure. We're about to solve mysteries in their private, little universe. And to them, it's important. I'm sorry for coming at you like a runaway freight train. I just know you're very busy, and your time is limited and important."

"Well, that's it for me. Questions, anybody?"

"Reach out if you need help or have concerns. I'm all in. I plan to rock these boys' world. And I know we can and will."

"All right. Go knock their socks off at your house with a fantastic dinner. I'm here for you. Don't forget that. Call me before you panic. Have a great evening, ladies."

"And don't forget to laugh. Sometimes, I feel like a deer standing in the middle of the road, blinded by the headlights, with a loaded dump truck bearing down on me. The key is to keep moving."

"I'll talk to you tomorrow."

Mom's call went flawlessly. There was never a doubt in my mind.

CHAPTER 6
Research Bonanza

(Mom/Mrs. Betty Johnson)

Late Monday Afternoon

I called the Highlands Herald newspaper office after finishing the moms' team FaceTime call. The customer service receptionist forwarded my call to the archives data services department, which handles inquiries. The nice man was polite and listened to the whole background story before reacting.

"Mrs. Johnson, I'm sure I can help you with your name search, but I'd like you to speak with someone on our editorial staff first. Would you mind telling them what you've just told me?" Robbie (Mr. Taylor) asks. "I think it might make a great human-interest article that could, in mere days, get local citizens to share what they know or remember."

"I'd be more than happy to, Mr. Taylor," I reply.

Robbie Taylor seemed perfectly suited to his data services role. He'd apprenticed at the Herald during college, and the newspaper offered him a permanent job after graduation. His work schedule allowed him to moonlight in the evenings as a web designer and consultant.

I was on hold while Robbie called the editorial desk. He evidently had to explain why he was forwarding my query call to the editorial department, but in three minutes, I was speaking to the editor-in-chief, Mr. Baker.

"Hello, Mrs. Johnson. My name is Simon Baker. I've been told you have a very unusual story that may be of public interest. I'd love to hear what you shared with Mr. Taylor. Afterwards, I'll tell you how I think we can help. Does that sound reasonable?" Mr. Baker exclaims.

"Absolutely, Mr. Baker. Would you prefer I do it over the phone now?" Mom asks. "It will take about 5-10 minutes."

"Why don't you give me your 5-minute version, and I'll decide whether I need to book a longer session for you in the morning," Mr. Baker says.

"I'll try, Mr. Baker," Mom replies.

"My son Timmy, he's twelve, went tree-climbing in Baker Park last Saturday. He found a sardine can tied to a tree limb in an old oak tree. Duct tape and rope kept the can secure and hidden. All of it was very weathered, showing it might have been there for years. It contained a folded note wrapped around an old coin. Timmy brought it home, deciphered the water-stained note, identified the old Spanish coin, and showed them to us at the dinner table. Johnny Butler wrote the note in 1968. The Army drafted him and probably sent him to Vietnam. The coin is a 1678 Spanish Real. Johnny said in his note that his middle school history teacher gave it to him."

"Timmy shared the story with friends in his Sunday School class. Now they're excited and curious about Johnny Butler. Was he a hero? Did he get a medal? Where is he now? And many other questions. So, all the boys' moms are helping research public records to find out more about Mr. Butler," Mom concludes.

"Well, Mrs. Johnson, I'm curious myself now. Can I ask a favor of you?" Mr. Baker asks.

"Ask away," Mom replies.

"I'd like to get together with you in person for a group session with my section editor and his lead reporter, preferably tomorrow. We'd like to see Johnny's note and the coin, and anything else that you feel might be helpful to us. My staff will want to get names and more story details and find out what the boys are hoping to get from this research. They will want to meet the boys and tap into their curiosity and excitement, too," Mr. Baker says.

"I'd be more than happy to do that. How about 10 o'clock?" Mom asks.

"I'll set it up, Mrs. Johnson. Anything else you want to add?" asks Mr. Baker.

"Well, I'm having the boys over for dinner tomorrow to give them an update on the research we're doing," I tell him.

Mr. Baker responds, "You're kidding, right?"

I could tell by the tone of his voice he was beaming, elated at this fortuitous turn of events. "No joke, Mr. Baker. I set it up with the boys yesterday afternoon." It was so encouraging to imagine his interest spiking as much as ours.

"Thanks, Mrs. Johnson. I can't wait. I look forward to seeing you tomorrow. Our lobby receptionist will let us know you're here, and I'll send staff downstairs to escort you to my boardroom. Have a great evening."

"I'll see you tomorrow. You have a nice evening as well, Mr. Baker," mom replies.

Mr. Baker has been the editor of the Herald for over 20 years. And his newspaper career probably goes back another 20 years before that. Can you imagine him getting down in the weeds with our story like this? That says a lot about his commitment.

***

It's time to start dinner, but I need to text an update to the other mothers first. Let's build some momentum and enthusiasm. Go, team!

Group text: Ladies! A quick update. I contacted the newspaper staff today. I gave them the story of Johnny Butler's hidden note, the coin, and our boys' excitement and desire to learn more and perhaps meet Mr. Butler. The editor-in-chief wants to see the coin and note and discuss story possibilities. They might want to interview the boys tomorrow night. That's just a hunch, since I told Mr. Baker the boys were coming over for dinner and their first Johnny Butler research update.

***

I laid out a German-style dinner this evening. It wasn't in my recipe book of family favorites, but I can pull it out twice a year with no risk of backlash.

"Time to wash up for dinner, guys, it's on the table," Mom announces. Dad and I were both tuned in. I know I was. I finished my homework and was playing a game on my PlayStation. Dad was off work yesterday and today because he'd worked last Saturday.

We got to the table at the same time. Mom was already standing next to the table, and I think Dad came from the recliner in the living room. We both lined up at the sink to wash and dry our hands. Then, we all sat down together.

This was a DIY meal. After Dad's family prayer, we all reached for the nearest bowls and platters, then politely passed them around to each other until everyone had gotten a portion of everything. It was nothing like the pre-teen mayhem that ensued at the table yesterday with my friends. Our family table manners seemed well rehearsed and organized. But it was simply our normal routine. We just called it learning table manners and practicing them.

Our table conversation was light this evening since Dad had the day off and was home all day.

Mom mentioned she did a FaceTime call with the other mothers and then called the newspaper office to get their help to research any mention of Johnny Butler. She didn't go into detail but said they would help, and that she was going to speak to them again tomorrow morning. She asked me if she could borrow Johnny's note and the coin, so they could see them. That seemed logical. No problem.

Then Mom added, "Don't forget to remind your friends that they're eating dinner at our house tomorrow, just as we planned yesterday. Tell them to be here by 5:30. And remind them to encourage their moms to come, too, if they are available."

After dinner, I went to my room and texted Tommy and Sam about Mom's message to remind the guys, just as she'd asked. I also walked over to Ted's house and gave him Mom's message. (I couldn't text Ted because he'd lost his phone privileges for three days. Ted's parents are strict and set a limit on his phone privilege. He pushed his luck too far. Sometimes, we stubbornly learn the hard way).

The wheels are turning, or should I say 'churning.' I'm sure the guys will be glad to hear that. I think the newspaper archives are our best hope for finding Mr. Butler. I wonder what they will think of our story.

"Hey, Mom," I imparted across the hall at bedtime. "I called the guys and told them what you asked me to. It should all be fine."

Sometimes, I wonder how all the players and moving parts work together when we're not in the same location. Keep things simple, communicate clearly, and trust that everyone does what they're supposed to, precisely when it's supposed to happen.

It's just like a baseball game. You play your position, have your spot in the batting order, and do your part. It's not magic, it's teamwork!

CHAPTER 7
Newspaper Home Run

Tuesday

I see my first-period teacher, Ms. Sheridan, in the hall just outside the classroom door before class.

"Good morning, Ms. Sheridan," I exclaim with syrupy politeness.

"Good morning, Tim. I'm glad to see you. Can I speak with you in private? It'll only take a couple of minutes," she promises.

"I guess so, Ms. Sheridan. Am I in some kind of trouble?" I ask.

The first-period bell rings, leaving us in the hallway alone. I'm nervous as she steps between me and the door. My first thought is, 'This can't be good.'

"I heard Tommy and Sam talking to a couple of their friends yesterday," Ms. Sheridan says. "They were very excited and said they were in a new gang, and you were in it, too. It's none of my business, but I wanted to share my concern and maybe get some clarification. The word 'gang' has a terrible connotation to it and causes many people to shy away or even steer clear of you out of fear. Can you help me out? I'd like to understand," Ms. Sheridan explains.

"I don't mind at all, Ms. Sheridan. It's nothing bad like that at all. It's not a gang of bullies, thieves, or even vandals. Not at all. It's just a club. We were climbing a tree on Saturday, and Sam said we should call ourselves the Treetop Gang. That's all," I clarified. "It's not even an actual club. There are no rules. We just like hanging out together and dig climbing trees."

"Well, that eases my mind. I'm so relieved. I wasn't eavesdropping, but what I overheard was troubling. I appreciate your honesty, Tim," Ms. Sheridan replied as she put her hand on my back and ushered me into the classroom.

Everyone in the class was curious and watching as I came in and took my seat. I suspect my smile just added to their bewilderment. It would distract them, at least until the end of the period.

*** Mom ***

"Hello, Mrs. Johnson," Mr. Baker exclaimed. He was already sitting in the boss's chair at the head of the boardroom table, with two gentlemen and a young lady nearby, when the secretary ushered me in. He stood, out of respect, then proceeded.

"Let me introduce you to Robbie Taylor, from our archives data services department, who you spoke with yesterday. The gentleman to my right is Mr. John Nyles, our city desk editor. And this young lady beside him is Ms. Sarah James, his best staff writer. She'll be helping John capture the key elements of your story and plan our coverage. They will also track Mr. Taylor's research for mention of Mr. Butler in our archives, which also encompasses obituaries."

"Please have a seat. Do you want some coffee, a soft drink, or a bottle of water? All of you, please. Help yourselves. It's all on the buffet table," Mr. Baker states as he gestures to his right with his arm extended.

"Did you bring the coin and Johnny's note for John and Sarah?" Mr. Baker asks.

"I'm delighted to meet you all. Yes, I remembered. Here they are," Mom replies.

I placed the coin, wrapped in a tissue, Johnny's original letter, and the deciphered text of his note. (I also brought out the contact list, research assignments, and the notepad with the boys' questions, which I kept beside me for the time being.)

They passed the items amongst themselves for about three minutes before pushing them to the middle. Then they turned their attention to me, first thanking me for sharing the items, then asking me to retell the story in as much detail as possible, along the actual timeline, so they could track what transpired and capture the five W's and one H of a good story. (Who, What, When, Where, Why and How)

Mr. Baker excused himself and graciously bowed out to attend to other business. I did as they requested. My 5-minute synopsis for Mr. Baker yesterday grew to a 25-minute detailed story for John, Sarah, and Robbie. They were taking notes as I spoke. After I finished, they had several questions for me:

What about the boys' interest inspired you to act?

How much information do you think you can glean from public records?

Are the boys aware that Mr. Butler holds the key to many of their questions?

Finding Mr. Butler alive, healthy, and willing to meet and talk to the boys is the best-case scenario. Do they understand he may be older than anyone they know and may, heaven forbid, be deceased?

We can predict that readers will respond to our story with facts that may or may not be accurate and leads that could be dead ends or present new research challenges. Are you working towards a hard deadline?

How much work are you planning to put into this?

How far has this story circulated?

We'd like to interview the boys for their perspective and assess their expectations and hopes firsthand. Mr. Baker said you had a research update planned with the boys. Could we interview them after your update? It would take about 30 minutes. And we'll need signed consent forms if we attribute any statements to specific boys. It's likely we'll want a group picture as well.

There could be other media interest in this project, too, once we publish our story. I'm comfortable saying our target release day is this Thursday.

Are you okay with us pitching this story to our affiliate network channel?

I responded to every question. I asked for, and they gave me, ten consent forms. I asked if the forms were self-explanatory, contained any restrictions, such as non - disclosure, and what liabilities we would face if we spoke to someone without prior authorization. They assured me they would go over all that this evening.

Our boardroom exchange ended at 11:30. They each gave me their business card and told me to call with questions, plan changes, or research updates.

I gave them my cell number and our address for the dinner at 5:30 and the Johnny Butler update afterward.

Boy, oh boy. Talk about starting strong. I'd better hustle home. Our Next FaceTime call is staring me in the face. It's a mere two hours away now.

***

"Hi, ladies. I'm so grateful you could all be on board today. I'm eager to get your input, but first, I need to clue you in on my sessions with the Highlands Herald staff from yesterday and today."

I gave them a recap of my phone chats with Mr. Taylor and Mr. Baker, and then with him and his staff this morning. Then I covered their desire to talk with the boys this evening, filling out consent forms, outlining privacy protections, addressing liability, etcetera.

Casey said she did name searches on Facebook and Instagram. The John/Johnny/Johnathan Butler profiles that were found didn't match the age of our J. Butler.

Bonnie reached out to the local American Legion and VFW posts. Neither organization was operating in Highlands in 1968. Current membership rosters have no John/Johnny Butler. We can search for past members, but only at the national level. The commander will see what he can do. He usually calls back in a day or two.

Lisa contacted the county school board. She got a list of schools operating from the 1950s to the late 1960s. Lisa requested a name search for Mr. Butler, but the staff member was reticent. She questioned our need to know and cited privacy regulations. Lisa then mentioned it should be public information. The school board representative offered to arrange a meeting with the superintendent tomorrow.

"Ladies, I think we've made some significant progress. I appreciate your efforts. It would be so encouraging if you could make it for dinner tonight. Bring the boys' siblings, too, especially if that's all that's stopping you. Just text me a head count, so I'm prepared."

"I think you will benefit from listening to the dialogue between the reporter and our boys. And I'm sure Ms. James will answer questions you may have, too."

"It's 2:30. Kids will be home from school soon. Dinner is at 5:30. I've got it covered. Give me your headcount, and I'll take it from there. Thanks again, ladies. Please come. Please. Bye."

***

The moms got back to me. Our dinner headcount is 18. I plan to seat the four boys at the kitchen table, set up the living room with two six-foot folding tables and 12 chairs for guests,

59

and will use the dining room table for the reporter, photographer, curious spouses, and any surprise guests.

I will use two air fryers, the toaster oven, and the range oven to heat ten pounds of chicken nuggets and eight pounds of fries. I'll open two one-pound bags of carrot sticks and a one-pound bag of celery sticks and set out three bottles each of Ranch dressing and ketchup on the counter. The plan is set and in motion. Let's do this, Betty! I think to myself.

***

"I'm home, Mom. How's everything going? How did the meeting with the newspaper people go?" I ask.

I encountered unexpected silence, unusual for my mom. She's always cheerful and even bubbly.

A minute later, she says, "Hi, hon. It all went well. I can use your help to set the tables. I'd really appreciate it."

"No problem, Mom. I got this!" I reply.

I went to work immediately. I set out plates, napkins, and plasticware, and I placed a red Solo cup on each place setting. I set out a plate of carrot and celery sticks and a bottle of Ranch dressing and ketchup on each table. I set three buckets out on the kitchen counter (for ice), not to be filled until 5:30. It was 3:30, and the house was ready. Game on! Let the show begin!

***

Ms. James and a newspaper photographer arrived at 5:10. "Welcome, Sarah. We didn't really have time to speak this morning. I hated it was so formal," Mom offered. "How long have you been doing this?"

"Meetings all go that way unless you're in the break room. Sorry," Sarah added.

"I've been reporting for almost nine years now. I loved it so much in high school. I majored in journalism at college. The pay isn't the greatest, but I didn't get into it for that, anyway. I enjoy meeting people, covering civic events, and doing stories that enrich people's lives, like this story."

"Well, I hope you get all the information you'll need for the article tonight. Just ask if you think anything is being left out," I advised her.

"I will, Mrs. Johnson. You're very kind, and we appreciate you inviting us into your home," Sarah concludes.

***

My friends and their families came cruising in ten minutes later. The latecomers were here by 5:40.

Mom corralled everyone behind their chairs, gave some general instructions, and asked everyone to bow their heads for prayer. She asked the blessing, which was a tremendous relief to me. I could already hear the snickers and feel the elbow jabs. You know how guys can be. But I would have prayed if Mom had asked me.

All the moms insisted on helping. They put out baskets of warm chicken nuggets and fries on all the tables, then went around with the ice buckets, sweet tea, and fruit punch. Everyone was on their own after that.

The talking was loud, but not deafening. To my surprise, no one spilled their drink, were courteous about getting refills, and threw their paper plates, plasticware, and cups in the trash bin when they finished. Sarah said she thought we had probably rehearsed this. There's that word again. But we live by cafeteria rules. It's our daily routine. It's repetition. Musicians and actors 'rehearse.'

Duh!

After eating, the moms picked up leftovers and condiment bottles and brought them all back to the kitchen counter. The moms put the chicken and veggies in storage containers. They put the tea, punch, condiments, and containers in the fridge.

Once the kitchen was tidy, Mom herded us back into our seats. She proclaimed it was now, officially, time for our first

Johnny Butler research update. She turned and motioned for Sarah and Ben, the photographer, to step forward, then introduced them as Highlands Herald staff. Mom said they were here to observe and take notes and photographs for an article on our Johnny Butler story. She also mentioned that Sarah wants to get our thoughts on the mysteries we want solved. Following that brief introduction, Sarah and Ben took their seats.

Mom was up first. She talked about her contact with the people from the newspaper, their archive searches and her interest in an article for the public that might lead to reader information about Johnny, his teachers, classmates, relatives, acquaintances, fellow soldiers, etcetera. She said she'd let Sarah speak last so she could add what the article would cover, ask questions that might be good to include in the article, and answer questions we might have for her.

Casey, Bonnie, and Lisa each gave their research findings. They emphasized these were their initial contacts and most would require follow-up calls.

At some point, I recognized that kids and adults were clapping as each speaker wrapped up their research summary, and Mom thanked them. It was an unanticipated recognition that I'm sure touched our mothers' hearts. And it probably registered with Sarah as well.

Can you believe it? My friends are courteous, well-mannered, grateful, and sincere. And they're guys!

Then Sarah stepped forward. She asked if parents had signed the consent forms, collected them, and then asked the parents if they had questions about whether they were legal documents and if they restricted the boys or parents from sharing the story at church, school, work, etc. She said it was a boilerplate document the newspaper needed before telling our story. This protected the newspaper from potential lawsuits in the future.

Sarah read our story, as she understood it, from her notes from Mom's visit to the newspaper office this morning. She wrote a detailed and concise story. She even captured what we hoped to accomplish by searching for records of Johnny Butler.

She then pulled out Mom's list of questions each boy shared around the table on Sunday afternoon. She said they'd record our round-table discussion this evening, since she'd be busy moderating. Sarah went around the table, just like Mom did, talking to each boy one at a time. She read each boy's questions, then asked if he had thought of any more in the last two days. She then asked about us literally meeting and talking to Mr. Butler and how that would make us feel inside.

It took her 35 minutes to complete the cycle. She then told everyone she'd be completing the article tomorrow, and it would be in Thursday morning's edition. She said she had talked to their TV network affiliate, and they would like to read a copy of the article before committing to a feature on our story and search for Johnny Butler.

She then said both media releases would generate a lot of public response. She said that the newspaper story alone would generate, typically, about 100-200 responses. Network broadcasts, depending on the day of release and length, could generate up to a hundred more responses. Many will be cordial 'thank you' messages acknowledging the heartwarming story, and a percentage will be factual info on Johnny or just leads about when they last heard from, about, or saw him.

The big takeaway was that information was going to come in quickly, so be ready. The newspaper will cover your story; however, lead follow-up, sorting, and analysis fall to us. The same applies to the TV affiliate. Both will want to do a back-end closing piece, so be prepared for that, too. Once it's in the public domain, a lot more people would want to know about what happened to Johnny Butler. However, their interest stems from curiosity, unlike our more personal stake.

Sarah then let Ben do his thing. He requested mothers form a line; their sons were told to stand in front for a group photo. After taking the shot, he wrote everyone's names in the order they'll appear in the caption under the photo -- back row, left to right, then front row, left to right. His next photos were a close-up of the coin, front and back, and then Johnny Butler's deciphered note. Then he took a fifth photo of me holding the original note and coin, one in each hand. His sixth and final photo was of the Treetop Gang. He said these photos won't all be in the print edition, but Sarah would choose based on which would go best with the details of her article.

Ben's role was much more intriguing to me than Sarah's. He was running the recorder, holding a boom microphone, operating the camera, changing lenses, and taking notes. Everybody got the sense he was the magician in the act. He never stopped until they were ready to pack up and leave.

After Sarah and Ben left, I was relieved and excited. I think we all were. We all knew we would go on with our typical daily routines, but it felt like that might be harder to do now. School and responsibilities will still demand our attention. And our moms will still do their mom things. But Johnny Butler was now a part of our consciousness. What is he doing right now? He's about to be shocked out of his shoes!

***

The media and public barrage that Sarah described was borderline terrifying. We had never given an interview or been the subject of a newspaper article before. And no TV station had ever taped any of us for a story, which Sarah said would probably happen within the next few days. It might seem overwhelming, but many things are. Yet, like all of life, it all happens one day at a time. One encounter at a time. For now, we will go to bed and get our rest. School tomorrow. More research by our moms. And wait.

"Good night, Mom. Thanks for all you did today. I love you."

"Good night, honey. We've had a good day. Let's be thankful. God is good," Mom concluded.

"I couldn't agree more."

"I love you, too, Timmy. Sleep well," she added.

I can't wait for Thursday to get here! But there's no other choice!

CHAPTER 8
What's Normal Anymore

Wednesday

Breakfast was routine, and so was the bus ride to school. And that's about where anything like normal said adios. You could almost feel the amped-up electricity in the air. The pace and tempo in the halls were quicker. There were smiles. A lot of smiles. And shoulder bumps. Give me a break! What's going on? Did someone stick a 'Super Nerd' sign on my back?

I'm willing to bet one of my pals told somebody, who told somebody else, that newspaper people came to my house, talked to all of us, and took a lot of pictures. I can just hear them! 'Hey! Guess what? There's going to be a newspaper article about us in the Herald tomorrow!'

Sandy is standing beside my locker. I can see her from the other end of the hall. Oh, boy. Secret crush meets 'the shy guy.' This ought to be good. Will he crash and burn? Stay tuned. Details in two minutes!

"Hi, Tim. It's good to see you," Sandy began. "I was just wondering. Would you come and sit with me and two of my friends at lunch? We want to ask you a couple of questions. Your name has been popping up a lot lately. Did you know that? I think it's cool. Oh. And I promise. We won't embarrass you."

"I'd love to eat lunch with you, Sandy. Thanks for the invite. I'll see you later." Of course, my heart is racing as my thoughts run the gambit of what-ifs. Top of my list is, What if she likes me?

My first two classes seemed routine. Sam and Tommy were in my first-period class, and Ted was in my second-period class. We glanced across the room a couple times, but we couldn't speak, so we just nodded. Ted raised his cell phone once and pointed to it, but there was no way I was going to risk reading a message or texting him during class.

Sandy and Bernie, one of her friends, are in my third-period class. Sandy gave Bernie's arm a light touch as she slightly nodded her head in my direction, just as they came through the door. Bernie raised her eyebrows, with a slight grin on her lips, acknowledging me, then leaned her head over closer to Sandy and whispered something. That certainly made me feel awkward. Did she say something good? Nice? Funny? I can only hope, but my first instinct is always dread. Is there jelly on the corner of my mouth? Is there toothpaste on the front of my shirt? It happens!

The self-deprecating negativity is probably a signature trait of underlying insecurities. Did that psychology gibberish just come out of my head? I'm sorry. Did I get any of it on you? Or me?

Honestly, though. I'm more than fine around guys. But girls tear my stomach up. I'm cornered, and I panic. Breaking the ice is like facing lions with a steak in my hand. Loser!

We always think the worst. We fear ridicule. We're kids, self-conscious kids. It follows us around.

***

My sense of 'normal' was still trying to leave the building. I notice the oddest thing walking through the cafeteria line. My Tuesday evening dinner is being served as our Wednesday school lunch. Déjà vu! Coincidence? Maybe. But all I'm thinking is, 'this is squirrelly,' Tim Johnson. 'Beam me up, Scottie!' I'm in a new time and dimension.

I grabbed an apple, a carton of chocolate milk, and a bottle of water on my way out of the cafeteria line. As I look around, I see Sandy, Bernie, and Sofie sitting at the end of a table near 7-8 other girls. Technically, they were sitting alone. It just didn't seem that way to me. Instead of feeling elation, I'm nervous and on guard. It almost feels like I'm trespassing. This is girl turf. No boys allowed!

Then, as I look around, I see Tom, Sam, and Ted with other guys at the last table by the back wall of the cafeteria. They're all staring at me; a few are pointing, and others have hands over their mouths, trying to cover a grin, smirk, or chuckle.

This is all so wackadoodle.

As I set my tray down, we each say hi, hoping it lightens the uneasiness that I know I'm feeling. Sandy seems to be in charge on her side of the table, cool, calm, and collected, as people like to say. Since I'm sitting alone on my side, Sandy takes the lead and starts the conversation.

"We hear you like to climb trees, Tim," she declares. "Have you ever seen any girls climbing trees?"

"I haven't, but that doesn't mean girls don't climb trees," I responded. "Why do you ask?" This line of inquiry was unexpected. Need I add, bizarre!

"We heard Ted and Sam talking to some of their friends about their tree-climbing club, the Treetop Gang. They said you and Tom were in it, too. We've never heard of a tree-climbing club and were wondering if it's just for guys," Sandy replies. "And why do you like to climb trees? What do you get out of it?" she added.

"Well, Sandy, let me explain. It's not an official club, and there are no rules. We were just out climbing an old oak tree together last Sunday, and the name just popped into Sam's head and straight out of his mouth. None of us objected. We just went along with it. We haven't had time to climb since then."

"As for answering your 'why' question, let me give it a try," I tell them. "I've probably climbed trees for 4-5 years. It's usually quiet in the trees, and it's a great place to read, dream, imagine, pretend, and just relax. Sometimes, I'll watch the squirrels and birds or the clouds as they drift across the sky. Sometimes, I might even text or take pics. I've even eaten my lunch in a tree before. Solitude helps me find peace when the busy world just wants to pile on more 'stuff.' I get to 'check out' for a while. Trees are my friends. And they like me. It's just a feeling, I know, but it feels good."

"Wow. Thanks, Tim," Sandy replied. "That's a very personal observation. Let me throw you a curve ball now. Is that okay? What would you think if we said we'd like to try it, tree-climbing? Would you teach us how to climb and what to watch out for? I'm not sure we'll even like it, but we're curious and would like to find out."

"I'd be glad to show you what I've learned and the things I watch out for. When would you want to try it? I usually go to Baker Park on Saturday mornings. Would that work for you?" I ask.

Hey, bud. Did all of that just come out of your tongue-tied mouth?! You'd better watch yourself. Tim doesn't do 'smooth' around girls. Remember?

Sandy and the girls all put their heads together. They popped out of their three-girl huddle, all smiles. Bernie then says, "We'd like to try it this Saturday, maybe at 10 o'clock, if you're okay with that."

"All right, then, ladies. It's a date. Wear jeans, a T-shirt, a long-sleeved shirt to protect your skin, and some comfortable shoes. Tennis shoes, hiking boots, or even high tops are fine. Tree bark is rough, so if that concerns you, bring some leather, canvas, or thick rubber gloves, too. Questions?" I ask.

"I think we're all fine, Tim. If anything should come up, we can ask you on Saturday," Sandy proclaims.

"Well, let me give you my cell number. You can text or call me if anything comes up. Just a heads up, though. If it rains, I don't climb. Safety is a big part of fun," I tell them as we empty our trays and exit the cafeteria.

Slick trick, there, Tim. Slide your cell number across the table to three girls, all at the same time. You're one sly dog, man!

"Thanks for inviting me to lunch, Sandy."

Boy, did that catch me off guard. What would make a girl curious about climbing trees? I'm sure a couple of my cousins climbed trees when I first got started. In fact, both were older than me at the time and probably taught me most of the 'ropes.' (Dang it! How could I forget that? I need to share this with the girls!)

So now it's my turn. I can now, years later, return the favor my cousins showed me.

I hope the other guys in the club don't have a fit, object, or drop out. And frankly, it's not like the girls asked to join our club. But what if they had? Would that be a big deal?

We'll see.

CHAPTER 9
Hot Off the Press!

Thursday

I can't believe it. Our Johnny Butler story is in the paper!

Mom has the paper on the breakfast table open and folded so the article is visible. "Can you believe this, Mom?" I exclaim. "It hasn't even been a week since I found his note and coin."

When I get to school, I see it on my first-period teacher's desk. Our principal, Mr. Jordan, sees me in the hall, and he tells me he liked our story and hopes we find Johnny.

All the Treetop guys are standing at my locker as I pass by there between the first and second periods. Are they as shocked as I am? We're bent over, heads down, standing in a circle, whispering. Other kids are pointing and whispering. It's eerie. They look at us like we're celebrities or, God forbid, freaks, but we're just kids doing kid stuff. This is so crazy.

"Hi, Sandy," I remark as she and Sofie walk past me in the hall. "I hope you have a great day!"

"Hi, Tim," Sandy replies. "I hope you do, too. See you at lunch?"

"I'll drop by. See you then."

Oh my gosh! That was completely more than I'd planned or expected. I decided I'd be more outspoken now since we'd broken the ice over lunch yesterday.

All budding friendships start with being open and friendly, right? You can check that box, Tim!

Wait a minute. Have I sprouted some stud muscles? Is Tim the school's hot, new, chick magnet? Nah! Nice dream, though.

Our lunch encounter was brief. The girls were at their usual table. "Hey, ladies. I thought I'd stop by and say hi," I said. "So, anything new going on?"

Sofie replied, "We heard there's a story in the paper about you finding Johnny Butler's note and coin in the tree at Baker Park. That's so neat."

"I still can't believe it myself. I hope it helps us find him," I say.

We affirmed we were still on for tree-climbing on Saturday. Sandy then mentioned all the chatter about the story and how some kids didn't even know about it yet.

"If you like, I'll get Mom to make copies for you. It would be a nice keepsake. She can probably have them ready by Saturday."

"We'd love that, Tim. That's so nice of you," Sandy replied.

I then excused myself so I could sit and gab with the guys. The balance of the school day was typical and uneventful.

***

Sarah gave Mom a courtesy call at 5:00 P.M. The gist of it went like this: We released the Johnny Butler human-interest story this morning. I hope you liked it. The Herald has never seen such an outpouring of interest. We received 167 daytime comments, which could double once evening reader responses come in.

She recommended we (Mom) reconnect with her tomorrow morning for an update and plan for follow-up actions. "Typically," she said, "print stories have a short life span, so comments may drop off just as quickly as they ramped up, but readers could stay interested and want to stay engaged, do some research on their own, and provide updates."

Can you believe that? I wonder. If 167 people commented, how many more read the story and didn't comment? I'm thinking, responses might come from less than three percent of total readers. So, if 167 people represents three percent of the readers, how many now know about my discovery and the Johnny Butler mystery?

I still can't imagine one Saturday tree-climbing adventure by myself turning into this gigantic hoo-ha. And it's probably just now catching fire.

Sarah's feedback and comments so blew my mind that I texted the guys to let them know. Kids never get this much public attention, if any. But truthfully, this story is more about Johnny Butler than four inquisitive kids wanting to find and talk to him. Now everyone wants to find and talk to him! It's like the cartoon 'Where's Waldo?' Everyone is on the hunt. And to think, just six days ago, it was just me and Mom! This is so nuts!

Friday Morning

Right after I caught the bus and headed off to school, Mom got a call from an associate program director at the TV station's satellite office. He said they read the Johnny Butler story in the Herald yesterday and agreed with their editorial staff that this story has great legs and will resonate with a wide swath of their viewing audience. He asked if he could send out a team on Saturday morning to meet Tim, film an interview with him, show the note and coin to their viewers, and then get some footage at Baker Park, where everything started. They'd also like to interview Mom and highlight the research angle and everyone's wildest hopes of finding Johnny. It seemed like a perfect plan, and Mom was on board. He assured Mom the team would be there at 10:00 A.M. and projected they'd probably be able to wrap up in an hour and a half max.

If Mom had only known I already had plans for 10 o'clock on Saturday morning. This is going to add a broader dimension to the story. And boy, are my friends going to be shocked. O-M-G! The club guys don't even know that girls are coming to learn how to climb, and the girls have no clue that there will be a film crew at my house, and they will now most likely have their own place on stage in the Johnny Butler quest. This is like bumper cars; you know the pile-up is coming, but when and how bad will it be? And will everybody be laughing when the ride is over?

Once I took all of this in, my brain went into overload, then overdrive. I told Mom about the girls and my plans to show them all I know about tree-climbing at the same time as the TV interview. She'd need to alert the TV station to the presence of three friends and see if that matters. Then I must call the guys and tell them about the girls' interest in tree-climbing, that they're coming over on Saturday, in addition to a television production crew. My plate is so full right now. Think, Tim.

What if they get upset, their moms get riled, and it causes a rift in our friendships and family relationships? I must warn Mom.

After talking to Mom, I immediately called Sandy and Ted to tell them that a TV crew was coming and there was a twist to our tree climbing plans. Sandy was elated, but Ted, not so much. He said he'd let the other guys know.

I've made no efforts to take the limelight, and view myself as nothing more than the accidental central character, the focal point for this still unfolding and snowballing story. But does everybody else see it that way?

I feel like I'm the only passenger on a runaway train, and there's no brake switch in my car. It's going to crash, and I'm too scared to jump. Oh, Lord!

***

Mom called Sarah at the Highlands Herald office right after her call with the associate program director at the TV station. Sarah was away from her desk, so Mom left a voicemail message. An hour later, Sarah called Mom.

"I'm sorry I missed your call earlier. I was in a meeting with my boss and Mr. Baker," Sarah explained. "Your story came up. They wanted an update. I told them there were 310 comments on your story and that the TV station said they'd be contacting you to set up a shoot for a 3- to 4-minute weekend feature, which will air on Sunday evening. So, Betty, what's your plans for tackling the comments?"

"It's been a busy morning, Sarah. The TV station called earlier and is coming out tomorrow morning. Thanks for calling me back. I'm excited about digging into the comments, but I'm thinking it might be Monday before I can do anything unless I can dig into them around lunchtime today. What would you suggest?" Mom asks.

"If you can come to the office in a while, I can hook you back up with Robbie. He can take you through the comments, sort out the more promising ones, and print them out for you. Can you make it around 11:00? I can let him know you're coming," Sarah adds.

"I appreciate your help, Sarah. I'll be there. It'll be nice to have a hard copy of the comments I can share with the boys and their moms. The 'team' can get to work culling through them over the weekend," Mom declared.

The weekend is going to be very 'event-full,' I mused, pun intended!

And Johnny Butler, where will this leave us? Are you ready for the shock of your life?

Friday Evening

"Whew. What a week this has been. Friday evening has never looked this good, maybe ever."

My school day was the closest to normal that it had been all week. Kids forgot about the newspaper piece, except for the girls, who still want a copy of the article as a keepsake. (I'll have to ask Mom to get some copies.)

The Treetop guys are coming over tomorrow, but they're not excited or giddy like the girls. Hopefully, they'll snap out of whatever it is.

"Hey! Want to go grab some pizza tonight?" Dad asked. "Tomorrow's shaping up to be packed."

Dad drove Mom and me to our favorite pizza restaurant for dinner. Eating out was Dad's way of giving Mom a break, a day away from the kitchen and housekeeping, and special thanks for doing so much.

"Dan, you're so sweet. You do more than your share for us. Please remember to remind me not to forget Father's Day," Mom said with a ribald chuckle.

"I'm just kidding, hon," Mom added. "And we won't even consider combining it with your birthday this year!"

The three of us can usually finish a large pizza between us, but tonight, I think we all had a good night's rest in the frontal lobes of our brains. We boxed the remaining three slices and headed home.

I called Sandy. That whim was becoming more predominant in my thoughts. "Hey, Sandy. How's everything going? Just wanted to check in and see if we're all still a 'Go' for tomorrow. I'm looking forward to it," I profess.

"We're excited and wouldn't miss it for anything, Tim," Sandy says. "I've got a hunch the weather won't be a problem since TV camera people are coming."

"Yeah. This wouldn't be a very good rainy-day story," I add. "Well, since it's getting late, I guess I should let you get to bed. See you tomorrow. Good night, Sandy."

"Thanks for calling, Tim. Good night," Sandy exclaimed.

My life is changing in so many ways. Johnny Butler, the mystery that he is, has propelled my world into hyper-drive. Come on, Saturday! Hit me with your best shot!

CHAPTER 10
Lives in 3-2-1!

Saturday Morning

Five people from the TV station showed up at 9:45. They all had Starbucks coffee cups in their hands and were in no apparent rush to get to work. That was just fine with me. I was more concerned about my friends' arrival and their reaction to the latest dog and pony show. I was so eager for everything to go smoothly.

Sandy, Bernie, and Sophie arrived right at 10:00. I called them (Sandy) last night to inform them of the camera crew that would also be there. As you can imagine, that just heightened their excitement. We stood around waiting for someone to step up and take charge. Well. Guess who? It was Mom!

Mom approached Mr. Nichols, the crew chief, offering the house's rooms. Following this, she invited the reporter to meet us kids.

"Hello, Mrs. Johnson," Ms. Arnold says. "Thank you for making time for us on such short notice. My name is Tonya. I'll be anchoring this segment. I would like to meet Tim so we can go over our planned monologue. Do you have any questions for me before we get underway?"

"Hi, Tonya," Mom replies. "I think we're dialed into your needs and will be as responsive as we can to your directions. Timmy had already planned to show some of his classmates how to climb trees safely this morning, so I hope that doesn't throw an extra monkey wrench into your plans. I think they'll just be excited to watch you from the sidelines while you do your work."

"We'll be fine, Mrs. Johnson," Tonya replies. "I'd like to start by getting some dialogue with you on tape about how the research is going. I've spoken with Sarah at the Herald, and she's given me some follow-up on their piece, so I'll ask you about that, too. Then I'll wrap your interview by asking you for some highlights of the boys' questions about Mr. Butler and public interest in the Johnny Butler mystery."

"We'll do several short 'takes' and splice it all together afterward. Then, we'll do the same with our short interview pieces with Tim. I'd just like you both to remember that you're talking to me and not the camera. The cameraman will track you on his own. You won't have to look for him. We'll then close Tim's piece with a tree-climbing snippet at Baker Park. It will all be quick, short, and sweet."

"We look forward to helping you and appreciate your station's interest in furthering public exposure to our adventure," Mom replies.

***

"Hi, ladies," I say to the girls as they get out of Sandy's mom's van. "I'm glad you made it. I apologize for this unexpected interruption. I don't think it will take very long."

The girls were ecstatic and perfect bystanders. There were smiles, whispering, and pointing. They were a pleasant distraction, though. Girls have become a new and mysterious phenomenon for me. And my former inhibitions are melting away.

Tommy, Sam, and Ted showed up about five minutes before Mom's interview concluded. I couldn't greet or speak to them because the TV crew was recording. The equipment crew ushered them over to the side where the girls were. Everyone knew each other from school, so there was no friction to deal with.

My interview was quick and painless. I'd answered the same questions for Sarah and described the discovery, note, and coin, just as I had several times before. The only thing left now was to head over to Baker Park and do what they asked for there.

***

Mr. Nichols started getting the crew and equipment organized for the short drive to Baker Park. Tonya told Mom they'd be going to the park to shoot their remaining takes. She invited Mom along if she wanted to watch. She declined, choosing instead to cull through the newspaper article comments.

The Treetop Gang and girls headed over to the park on foot. I had Ted lead the crew back from the park entrance to the back corner, where Johnny Butler's big old oak tree stands.

The guys weren't particularly interested in helping me teach the girls about tree-climbing, so I got the girls together off to a quiet spot away from everyone for a brief follow-up on our cafeteria session. My first course of business was to apologize.

"I'm so glad you're here today. I'm thrilled that you're interested in my favorite sport. First, though, I'd like to start off by apologizing," I told them.

Immediately, they looked at each other with astonished and bewildered stares.

"I told you yesterday that I'd learned to climb trees 4 or 5 years ago. But I didn't tell you who taught me. I had two teenage cousins that helped me learn the basics of tree-climbing. Their names were Tamara and Rachel. That bit of information is too important to leave out. They were tree-climbing girls! And that wasn't the totality of their outdoor skills, either. They could handle hammers, saws, ropes, and ladders. In fact, they were pros at building tree houses. They had sleepovers in their tree houses. That's important to know as you start your tree-climbing experiences. Girls can do much more than just climb trees. So now you know - it's not just a 'guy' thing."

"So, are you ready to test your strength? And brave the heights? You'll have some fear of heights and falling. We all do. That's natural. You'll eventually push those fears to the back of your mind, though. That's when tree-climbing becomes fun."

"Let's take a 15-minute break so that the TV crew can finish their filming. It shouldn't take long. Then, we can move on to the fun part. I appreciate your patience, ladies."

***

"Have your feelings changed about this tree after finding the note and coin and learning about Johnny Butler?" Tonya asks.

"It has given me a different perspective on aging, getting older. Johnny was 18 when he climbed this tree 50 years ago. He's my grandfather's age now. That blows my mind. And this tall, old oak tree was probably over 200 years old then and is at least 250 or 300 years old now. Both deserve a lot of respect. I think about that now when I'm climbing. This is a story about life and legacy, not just hanging out and having fun," I reply.

Tonya closed the segment with a typical reporter monologue. "Thank you for sharing your personal thoughts and feelings with our viewing audience, Tim. I can see this experience has already changed your life in some very profound ways. I hope you and your friends find Johnny Butler. It will affect his life in positive ways, too."

"If anyone watching this story knows Mr. Butler or might know of his whereabouts, please call or send us a message. Your help is so appreciated. For Channel Five News, this is Tonya Arnold, broadcasting from Baker Park in Highlands, New Hampshire. Have a good evening."

***

The guys had wandered off during the wrap of the closing interview. I felt the same way - this is grown - up stuff. And this is Saturday. We've got better things to do. A fire, wreck, or rescue would have been worth watching. But news stories are not usually geared for kids, and it's boring!

But, hey! The guys didn't even say bye, see ya later, be safe, or 'text us later.' I'm pretty sure they're miffed about something, but it's not like I can stop what I'm doing and run after them. And I'm very sure I wouldn't. Let them brood, for all the good that will do.

***

"Ladies! Are you ready to do some tree-climbing?" I ask. The departure of the TV station's grown-ups emboldened me to loosen up even more.

"I'd like to choose a tree that won't be too big and intimidating. We use the same skills and mindset for every tree, so rest assured, I'm not doing this because you are girls. If I had a brother or sister, I'd teach them the same things the same way. We'll start out easy and progress to the bigger and more challenging trees," I explain.

"Make safety your top priority with every step and hand and foot movement. Your first goal is not to fall. After a while, falling will be in the back of your mind, if not gone altogether, and safety will be second nature, instinctual. At first, tree-climbing will demand more focus and attention to detail and safety, and then it will morph into fun."

The first hour included multiple ascents, hand-eye-foot coordination, practice, practice, practice, assessments of tree limb strength, dialogue on fear of heights, pausing and scanning for pleasant views, descents, and then drops. I planned individual climbing instruction for every girl.

In the second hour, we climbed a more substantial tree. All four of us went up together. We stayed very close. I talked to all of them at once, reminding them of the basics—safety first, fun second. Don't forget. And remember, you're IN a tree, not lying under one.

We're able to share some views and point out birds watching us. Squirrels are below us and on branches in neighboring trees. At one point, Sandy noticed a rabbit at the edge of a meadow fifty yards away. Sofie and Bernie wanted to see it, but Sofie was on the opposite side of the tree and couldn't. It was a revealing lesson for all. Be vigilant. Never compromise your safety unless you're convinced that's the last thing you'll ever want to see in life.

After descending and dropping to the ground, I gathered everyone together and we reclined on our elbows, torsos bowed in a circular formation, facing inward. I felt I should provide a recap and get some feedback. It seemed awkward since we were all kids, but it seemed like this cake was worth icing. Bring it home, Tim!

"Ladies, I've had a wonderful time climbing my favorite trees with you today. I'm so glad you've tried this experience, and I hope it surpassed your expectations. You're all welcome to climb with me whenever you want. Remember the importance of safety, and the fun will come. It's a great place to be alone, whether by yourself, with friends, or an informal club. It's private, and peace of mind is yours free."

"Remember that tree-climbing is not a competitive sport. And it's not about showing off by taking risks. However, tree-climbing will keep your wits sharp, your body fit, and your mind relaxed. It helps us analyze problems, find solutions, and build resolve. Trees will become your friends, too. Of that, I'm certain. I apologize for the speech, ladies," I conclude. "It might be mushy, but I'll have this time we've had together today in my heart for a very long time."

All the girls, maybe shyer than I ever imagined, were speechless. They were clasping their hands over their hearts, wiping teary eyes, and scrambling to their feet. I got hugs I wasn't expecting. As they found their voices, they each thanked me, some with more words than others, but all with grateful and sincere hearts.

"Let's head to my house, ladies," I said as I walked with them out of the park. Can this day get any better?

Along the two block trek home, the girls are giddy and inquisitive. They ask for more details of the story they're hearing about the Spanish coin and note, what we've found out, and whether the article feedback gave us any new clues.

All I could say amidst the deafening clatter of speculative queries was, "Hey. Let's ask my mom for an update."

Mom knows how to make order out of pandemonium.

CHAPTER 11
Hello, Ladies!

Saturday Afternoon

Mom, true to her nature, was the hostess extraordinaire. She had finger sandwiches, chips, fruit punch, and cupcakes spread around the center of the table.

"Wash your hands, kiddos. I'm glad to see you're all back and smiling, cheerful, and all in one piece," Mom said. "Have a seat wherever you want. I can't wait to hear what you think of tree-climbing. But first, help yourselves. I hope you like it."

"You're so kind, Mrs. Johnson," Sofie said as the others added their assent.

Sandy then added, "We've had a great day, Mrs. Johnson. The TV interviews, Tim's tree-climbing lessons, hanging out, and now our very own brunch. It's all like a dream."

I then chimed in, "The girls would like to hear more about the Johnny Butler story, Mom. I've told them about climbing the old oak tree and finding the can, coin, and note. And they've heard about the newspaper story and seen the TV crew do its thing. What else can you add for them?"

"Well," Mom remarks. "First, take a few minutes to eat, chat, and relax. Then I'll bring out what I have."

Can you imagine where the conversation goes? Events at school are the hottest news of the day. Paula has a boyfriend. Josie has been out for two days. I wonder what's wrong? Did you see Marcy's outfit? I heard there's going to be a special school-wide assembly next week. Have you heard what that's all about?

There was nothing about tree-climbing. Zip! Nada!

Mom went to retrieve her folder and was back in a few minutes.

"Did you all have enough to eat? I didn't want to ruin your dinner," Mom said.

"Timmy. Why don't you bring down the Spanish coin, the original and deciphered notes, and the sardine can for the girls? I'm certain they haven't held them or even had a firsthand look at them yet," Mom added.

I whisked off to my room, retrieved them, then dashed back to the kitchen table. I divided them - can, coin, and notes, among the girls. They passed each item around, each reading the deciphered note and turning the coin over in their hands, marveling at the age of the coin and how many other people may have touched it over the past 350 years. Wow! We must all think alike!

Mom then begins, "There were 310 responses to the newspaper article. Mr. Taylor and Ms. James printed out the search results from their archives and the comments from the news story. I haven't gone through them thoroughly yet, but I can show you what I'll be sorting through. You can each look over a few sheets, and I'll summarize what I've gotten out of it so far."

"The first thing you'll notice on your sheets of paper is that many people just wanted to thank the newspaper staff for reporting a heartwarming story. Some asked if there would be a follow-up. Those comments make up most of the responses," Mom said.

"That leaves just 25-30 comments, out of 310, that might help us find Johnny Butler. Does that surprise you?"

"One commenter said he went to school with Johnny but didn't name the school or what year, or years, they knew each other. Another said he went into the Army with Johnny, but after boot camp, they didn't stay in touch. A third one said she heard that he'd moved out of State and gotten married but gave no specifics. Another one said he went to work for the government, but that's all he said. So, it gives us clues, but nothing solid. We'll be sending reply texts to follow up for more clarification."

Mom continued, "Robbie's summary of the newspaper archives was more helpful but offered no lead to his current whereabouts. There is no John Butler in the obituary files. That doesn't mean he's alive. It just means he hasn't died while living in our city or county. There was a clip of him passing his technical training after boot camp. He went to paratrooper school at Ft. Benning, Georgia, and earned his jump badge in September 1968. The article said he was still awaiting orders to his first duty station. There was no engagement, wedding announcement, or marriage recorded from local communities' news feeds, so it's safe to assume if he married, it occurred elsewhere and possibly out of State."

"So that's a very preliminary assessment of our progress. I'm hoping the school district archives can add more about him, but that will be before he left the coin and note, not afterward. It could, however, tell us who his parents were, whether he had any siblings or cousins, etcetera. That would point us to new contacts."

"I'm sure if you ask Timmy next week, he'll update you on the hunt for Mr. Butler. We're determined not to give up," Mom professes.

"So, ladies. Will I be seeing or hearing from you again? Are you still curious about tree-climbing? Was it too tough or scary?" Mom probed.

"We'll have to let you know, Mrs. Johnson. It's been a very 'different' Saturday for us, but in a good way. It's all been exciting and fun. But honestly, girls rarely do guy things and vice versa. The Johnny Butler story concentrates our interests, but in the end, we will have to decide individually what we take from it," Sandy said.

"I can appreciate that. I was never a tree-climber myself, other than following my big brother aloft a few times. It was just curiosity, I guess. I'm sure times have changed a bit since then. Well, please thank your parents for letting you come today. It's been a pleasure meeting you. You're welcome back anytime," Mom tells them. "I'm the only girl in this house, you know. That can make you feel lonely."

"And girls. Timmy said you all wanted a copy of the newspaper article. I've got one here for each of you. I laminated and slipped them into an envelope for each of you so they won't get wrinkled, torn or smudged."

"Thank you, Mrs. Johnson. You've done so much for us," Sandy said. "And thank you again, too, Tim. We rarely hang out with guys, but you're different. We like you. Enjoy your afternoon."

Sandy's mom is suddenly out front in her minivan. The girls all head out through the front door, then look back and wave as they pile in through the open sliding door. Bye, ladies! I will not lie. Your leaving is a downer.

Holy cow! Hearing 'We like you' from three girls in a lifetime, let alone in one day, is enough adrenaline surge to keep me awake for a week. There's no question in my mind of the importance of this day now. I need a group picture! Just the four of us. And I don't mean the Treetop Gang!

CHAPTER 12
Topping the Timbers

Sunday Afternoon

The Treetop Gang met at my house after lunch and wanted to head straight to Baker Park. Nothing of particular significance seemed on anyone's mind. At least, that's what I gathered from the general lack of conversation. But then I got the sense I was being left out of their three-way dialogue. Then, I knew something was bugging them. Something they weren't saying. This may have surfaced yesterday, but it has been simmering and festering even more since then.

Once again, just as I did the next-to-last time the four of us walked to the park, I came to an abrupt stop. I sat down on the curb with my back against the utility pole and crossed my arms. I waited and watched to see and measure their reactions. It registers with them. They know that I know something's up.

Then, finally, I say, "Guys. I don't know what people have said or what is going on, but we need to bring it into the open. I can't fix problems I'm unaware of. So how about if one of you starts this off? Tell me what happened, how you were wronged, and what I can do to fix it. Can you do that?"

Nobody wanted to go first or be the spokesperson, but Tommy reached deep, braved the audience, and spoke.

"Tim, I thought we were a club, the Treetop Gang. We're all best friends, and we have fun together all the time. We hang out at school. We go to Sunday School and church together. We text and share things with each other. So why did you think it wouldn't bother us when you invited the girls over to climb trees with you? You even ate lunch with them on Wednesday and didn't mention what was going on. Wouldn't you be wondering and upset?"

"Look, guys, I get it. I even worried about it as it was unfolding. But it happened quickly, along with a lot of other things, so let me break it all down for you if I might."

"On Wednesday, Sandy met me at my locker and asked if I'd eat lunch with her, Sofie, and Bernie. She said they had some questions for me. That's all she said. There was no chance for me to tell you before lunch. Sure, it was odd, but I didn't snub you intentionally. It just happened. It was quick and spontaneous."

"At the lunch table, Sandy said the three of them were curious about tree-climbing after they heard you say we were in the Treetop Gang, a tree-climbing club. They asked if I would teach them how to climb so they could see if they liked it. I said sure, I usually climb on Saturday morning, and they asked if they could come then. We planned everything, from start to finish, during lunch in the cafeteria. It never crossed my mind that I would need to ask your permission, and they weren't asking to join the 'Gang.' That never came up," I add.

"Well, why didn't you tell the TV people that we were the Treetop Gang?" Sam asked. "They just herded us over to where the girls were standing, and we felt left out. We didn't mind being spectators, but we started thinking we could find something better to do than being ignored and bored. And you barely acknowledged that we were even there."

"Well, guys, I can only say I was following instructions. And at that very moment, they wanted us all quiet. They were taping my mom's interview. And trust me, I wanted it over quickly. I thought you'd all understand and enjoy getting to watch the filming of interviews and the park sequences. I was trying my best to cooperate and get it over with," I profess.

"I certainly apologize for the misunderstanding, but it wasn't personal or intentional. Can we forgive and forget this whole incident? Talking things out is always better than letting issues simmer and fester."

Ted was the last to take the 'stand.' (I didn't know what to expect. I thought my last statement kind of closed the door on this total fiasco.)

"Tim, I've been your close friend longer than Tommy or Sam. I know you have a friendly nature and don't hold grudges or start fights. You don't start or tolerate rumors. You're a good example for all of us," Ted said. "That might have been what shocked us most over these last couple of days. It wasn't like you. And it wasn't normal. I really think the hubbub that's going on from this Johnny Butler story is getting to us all. We didn't really put our finger on it as fast as we should have. I believe you and apologize for questioning your intentions and behavior. You're the main reason we're all so close. So, what do you say? Let's get over to Baker Park and check on Mr. Green!" Ted exclaimed.

Oh, Lord. Did he just say what I thought he said?! How did he/they discover I'd named the old oak tree and talk to it? Where was the ribbing? What a great bunch of friends. The club is still intact.

I shouted, full of relief, "Thank you, Jesus!" as I clamored to my feet, hugging each of my buddies like it was a victory celebration. I think, for all of us, it was. We live to fight another day! Long live the Treetop Gang!

"So," Tommy announces. "I noticed there were only three girls that came on Saturday. Any chance they have another friend that enjoys climbing trees?"

There was a collective groan, but then raucous, gut-wrenching laughter. Girls climbing trees?! Who's betting it's just a way to meet guys?

Friends are a blessing. Need I say it? Cherish the ones you have. Ask the Lord to make you likable, more like Him every day. And, lest it slip your observation, ask for wisdom to abide their shortcomings, hurt feelings, and tempers. We're all human, after all.

The guys all head home, knowing it's probably close to dinnertime. It's always better to get home early than having your folks calling around to find you.

So, what's in store for Monday? Will it be a good day? And back to normal?

Oh, Lord. I've so forgotten the most important event of the day! Did I ever step in the poo this time! Was our Johnny Butler story even on the evening news?

Dang, it. That's a kid's life for you. Our focus and priorities differ completely from grown-ups. I hope Mom and Dad aren't mad at me for missing it.

I'm ready for Monday, Lord!

Take your best shot, world! I can handle it!

CHAPTER 13
He's Alive!

Sunday Evening

The local TV affiliate's coverage of the Johnny Butler story was a success. The public texted and called in responses in unbelievable numbers. Ironically, though, only one really mattered. Johnny Butler is alive. And he was watching the evening news and saw his own story. He lives 80 miles away in an assisted living facility.

Johnny was having dinner at a table with friends in the common area's main dining room when his story aired on Sunday evening. He immediately stopped eating and watched the story intently. The story shocked him, of course. He'd forgotten all about that little adventure until now. And to think, his hidden time capsule in the tree remained untouched for over half a century. That's so unbelievable.

He looked at his friends, who were looking at him, patting his back and touching his arm. They were astounded and curious, too. The entire country, it seemed, was looking for their friend, the man sitting right next to them, Johnny Butler. He was famous. And they knew him.

It was shocking to be the focus of so much attention, but he was ready to deal with it. Seeing the boy who found his note and Spanish coin intrigued and excited him. What a pleasure and joy it would be if they could meet. Would it be as special for Timothy Johnson as it will be for Johnny Butler? Johnny felt certain it would be.

"I'm ready to take this bull by the horns, Ms. Davis. Can you help me?" Johnny asked. He was standing, cane in hand, ready to go.

"You know I can and will help you, Mr. Butler," Ms. Davis affirms. "Just finish your dinner and let me know. There's no need to rush. We'll call from the office after you've eaten."

Johnny and Ms. Davis called the TV station right after dinner. Ms. Davis put the call on the speaker so no one had to contend with cell phones or poor reception. Unfortunately, the voicemail system answered their call. There were no front office staff working on Sunday evening at the TV station.

"Sorry, Johnny. We'll call them in the morning," Ms. Davis declares. "This will give us some time to let things sink in."

Farland is another of New Hampshire's smaller communities. It's half the size of Highlands in every way. They have one elementary school and a small high school. It has several healthcare centers and one Urgent Care clinic. There's one fire station, and the police department has just two police cars and six officers, including the police chief. It's probably safe to say that everyone knows everything that's going on.

***

Monday morning, after a good night's sleep, a warm breakfast and hot coffee, Johnny and Ms. Davis call the TV station again. The TV station's operator answers immediately and forwards their call to the program director.

"Hello? Mr. Terry? My name is Jennifer Davis. I'm the senior living coordinator at the Shady Retreat assisted living resort in Farland. I'm calling regarding your story last night about Mr. Johnny Butler. He's sitting here beside me. Do you want to speak with him?"

"I sure would, Ms. Davis. I appreciate your help in facilitating this call," Mr. Terry exclaims. "This is a dream-come-true moment for many people. I'm so thrilled to be the first to speak with him."

"Mr. Butler, my name is Abel Terry. I'm the program director at the TV station. Did you see the segment on the Johnny Butler mystery last evening? What do you think? Were you surprised?"

"Hello, Mr. Terry. It's a joy to speak to you. Surprised? I certainly was. Besides being shocked, I am so happy to learn a young boy found my note and that my favorite coin is now in excellent hands. I'd sure like to meet that boy. Of course, I can't climb trees anymore, but I think we'd have some stories to tell and maybe share some laughs," Mr. Butler confides.

"Mr. Butler, I want you to know the Highlands Herald did a human-interest story on you last Thursday, too. Did you see their article? Hundreds of people across the community responded and are interested in knowing more about you. They're wanting to meet you and hear your life story, too. Are you interested in that?" Mr. Terry asked.

"Well, that's a surprise to me, too. Nobody here mentioned it. I don't read newspapers myself anymore. My eyes aren't as strong as they once were. I might see the headlines and read a little, but other people tell me the news, and I watch it on TV," Johnny explained.

"I'd be fine meeting a few people, but I don't get out very much. I still have my driver's license, but I gave my car away when I moved here. The traffic just got too congested, and people were all in a hurry. I don't get in a hurry anymore. I have everything I need. But I'm sure we can arrange something, and I'd like that. If you want, you can work it out with Ms. Davis. She's my boss. I'll be fine doing what she says," Johnny added.

"Ms. Davis, I'd like to make some calls to the Herald and Mrs. Johnson, Tim's mother, before doing anything else. They know nothing about the responses to our segment yet. Once they're caught up, I'd like to coordinate some interview sessions, photo shoots and a short TV segment as follow-ups for our readers and viewers. We will, of course, weave in a personal meeting with Tim and Johnny in those arrangements, and I believe there are several friends of Tim who have a long list of questions for Mr. Butler about what he's been doing since 1968. Can I call you back later in the afternoon after I've made these initial contacts?" Mr. Terry asks.

"Certainly. We've enjoyed speaking with you."

"Johnny? Do you want to say or ask Mr. Terry anything?" asks Ms. Davis.

"I don't reckon I do right at this minute. I might try to find that newspaper article and read their story. I'll be ready when you want me. I'll be right here. Have a nice day, Mr. Terry," Johnny says.

"It's been a real pleasure speaking with you, Mr. Butler. If you can't find the article, I'll have it faxed over to Ms. Davis for you. Have a wonderful afternoon, Mr. Butler."

"I'll call you this afternoon, Ms. Davis," Mr. Terry promises.

"That'll be fine," Ms. Davis replies.

***

Mr. Terry, TV Program Director

"Simon? This is Abel. I've got an update on the Johnny Butler story we both covered. He's alive and living in Farland in an assisted living facility. He saw our news segment last night. I know little about his health, but he was on the phone during my conversation with the senior living coordinator there. He's lucid and articulate. He's interested in giving us follow-up pieces for our readers and viewers and wants to meet Tim and his friends."

"I wanted to give you a heads-up first. I'll call Mrs. Johnson next, and then we can strategize. I told Ms. Davis I'd call her back this afternoon. I'm hoping to get a better impression of Mr. Butler's health before we do anything that might be beyond his endurance. Is it okay if I call you in the morning, Simon?" Mr. Terry asked.

"Sounds like a good plan to me. I'm glad this outreach has paid off. I see a happy ending for many people. Thanks, Abel. I look forward to your call. Talk to you tomorrow. Bye," said Mr. Baker.

***

"Mrs. Johnson? This is Abel Terry from the TV station. How are you doing this morning?" he asked.

"I'm great, Mr. Terry. I enjoyed Tonya's segment with us that aired last evening. It's so amazing how the taping and splicing all come together so smoothly, and quickly," Mom adds.

"Thank you, Mrs. Johnson. We have good staff who take a lot of pride in their work. So, are you ready for some feedback? I know it's early, but I have some news," Mr. Terry proclaims.

"Oh, my! I'm always ready for good news. Is that what you've got?" Mom asks.

"It sure is. It's the best. Mr. Butler called me this morning. Can you imagine that? I was so shocked. He saw the story last evening as he was having dinner with friends. He'd like to meet Tim and his friends and probably see his coin and note one more time. He lives in Farland in an assisted living facility," Mr. Terry exclaims.

"Praise the Lord! Thank you, Jesus!" Mom shouts.

"You don't know how happy this makes me, Mr. Terry. If you were to ask my opinion, I thought these boys were betting on a long shot, a miracle. Fifty years is a long time. But I'm so happy to hear this. So, what's your plan, if I might ask?" Mom exclaims.

"Well, I called Mr. Baker first, then you. I told Ms. Davis, the coordinator at the assisted living facility, that I'd update everyone on our end and then get back to her this afternoon. I need to know if bombarding Mr. Butler with too much attention and excitement will jeopardize his health before proceeding. Once I know he's up to it, I'll get back to you and Mr. Baker, probably in the morning, and we can work on a strategy," said Mr. Terry.

"That's great, sir. I'm so happy. I need to update the other mothers assisting me, and the boys. Oh, the boys! They'll all be so excited. We can now end our research efforts thanks to your story. This has come together so fast. Tell Tonya I'm so happy for her. I hope she'll get to do your follow-up segment as well. Please forgive me. I'm just rambling now. I look forward to your call tomorrow, Mr. Terry. Have a spectacular day. Goodbye."

"I'll be in touch. Goodbye," Mr. Terry says as he hangs up.

***

"Ms. Davis. This is Abel Terry. Hope you've had a good afternoon. I contacted everyone on my shortlist in Highlands. How is Mr. Butler doing? I've got a pressing question I need to lead with. Is this revelation and public interest going to be too much for Mr. Butler? That's the main reason I wanted to call you back this afternoon. I wanted an opportunity to speak privately and candidly. We don't want to jeopardize his health or guilt him into overextending himself."

"I appreciate that, Mr. Terry. I'm happy to say Mr. Butler is one of our youngest senior residents living in Shady Retreat. He walks with a cane, but needs no other special accommodation. He's in great health. He's a widower. He no longer needed his large house and its maintenance. This facility meets his needs, cuts down his responsibilities and gives him the peace of mind he has earned and deserves. Having said all of that, he's as capable as any of the most able-bodied 70+-year-olds I can think of," Ms. Davis emphasized.

"So, I'd say, make your plans, draft an outline or summary, and let me review it. And better yet, if it would help, we could set up a conference call or a FaceTime session from our offices," she added.

"I think that's a splendid suggestion, Ms. Davis. What's the best time for you tomorrow?" Mr. Terry asked.

"I'd prefer 10:00 A.M., if that works for all the parties on your end. Our breakfast will be out of the way, lunch isn't until 12:15, and social workers will be directing activities for those who want to take part. Mr. Butler 'might' take part if it's pool or a card game, but we never have to worry about him. He's just as likely to be socializing, bird watching or meandering around the duck pond after breakfast," Ms. Davis exclaims. "He might even want to sit in on our call. Do you know if Timmy Johnson might be on the call? This could be a special occasion for the two of them," she adds. "I know Johnny's very excited about meeting this special tree-climber."

"I'm going to firm this up with everyone on my end before I leave for the day. We'll finesse our schedule to suit yours. Count on FaceTiming at 10:00 A.M. Please tell Mr. Butler we enjoyed hearing his voice earlier today and look forward to meeting him in person soon. By the way. Did you locate the Herald article for him?" Mr. Terry asks.

"We did. Thank you for remembering. He has read it, and it's on his dresser. I'm sure he'll look at it several more times and also share it at dinner with his friends. Have a great evening."

"You, too, Ms. Davis."

***

It's 4 o'clock, but I'm able to reach Simon and ask him to get his staff together for a four-way FaceTime call at 10:00 A.M. He said he'd be ready.

I call Mrs. Johnson and tell her what's planned for 10:00 A.M. tomorrow. I tell her that Mr. Butler would probably be on the call with Ms. Davis. I suggest that arranging for Tim to be on the call would thrill Johnny; they'd love to see Tim on camera, say hi, and talk to him.

We're set. That's the best we can hope for. It's going to be baby steps for the next few days. Mr. Butler's interests will direct us in what he can and wants to do and on his timeline

CHAPTER 14
What's Next?

Tuesday Morning

Mom says I can stay home from school for half a day. I heard that loud and clear!

We're going to FaceTime with a bunch of people while we sit at our breakfast nook. We'll be able to swivel the laptop left or right for individual shots or push it to the center of the table for a wide angle of us both. I'm going to have the coin, sardine can, and letter next to me in case Johnny wants me to hold them up for him to see. I wish I had a picture of our old oak tree, so he could see if he remembers it. I wonder if he has his own cell phone. I could take a picture and send it to him later.

***

The FaceTime call is a big-league accomplishment. Mr. Terry hooked up ten participants in four locations.

TV Station: Mr. Terry, Ms. Arnold, Ms. Maples

Highlands Herald staff: Mr. Baker, Mr. Nyles, Ms. James

Shady Retreat: Ms. Davis, Mr. Butler

Our House: me and Mom

"Hello, everyone," Mr. Terry started out. "It's 10 o'clock. I'm delighted to have everyone online this morning. Be aware of the camera angle when you're speaking so we can all see and hear each other. If you can mute your volume when you're not speaking, that will cut out distractions and any annoying background noise. Thanks for joining us. I'd like to start out with introductions since, for many, this is our first face-to-face chat."

"I'm Abel Terry. I'm the program director of Channel 5 TV. Ms. Tonya Arnold was our news anchor on the Sunday evening segment this past weekend. And Ms. Maples is my secretary. She'll be taking notes, dates, plans, and actionable items from this call and will ensure that participants get a copy. Simon, would you care to go next?" Mr. Terry asks.

"Sure, Abel. I'm Simon Baker. I'm editor-in-chief of the Highlands Herald. I have my City Desk editor, John Nyles, with me and his lead staff writer, Ms. Sarah James, who wrote the newsprint article in last Thursday's edition. We're excited to continue our coverage of this wonderful story. Mrs. Johnson? Please introduce yourself and the handsome young man next to you, if you would," Simon says.

"Good morning, everyone. My name is Betty Johnson, and this is my twelve-year-old son, Timothy. He's our tree-climber.

He found Johnny's note and mysterious, hidden treasure. His inquisitive nature has fueled this quest to find Johnny Butler and learn all we can about him," Mom says. "We're excited to be here and grateful to see Mr. Butler at last."

"Ms. Davis, please introduce yourself and the distinguished gentleman next to you there in your office, if you would," Mr. Terry interjects.

"Thank you, Mr. Terry. I'm delighted to put faces with names and hear your voices. I'm Jennifer Davis. I'm the senior living coordinator at the Shady Retreat assisted living resort here in Farland. Mr. Johnny Butler is alive, well, and sitting here right next to me. He's shocked by the notoriety this story has brought his way but loves socializing and can't wait to meet as many of you as he can, in person, over the next few days. I'll let him introduce himself now," Ms. Davis says.

"Hi, everyone. It's an honor to meet you all. I'm Johnny Butler. I'm not 18 anymore, as you can see. But I still remember a lot about growing up. You've made it sound like I've had an interesting life, so I hope I won't disappoint you. I just know I've had a good life and don't mind sharing my stories."

"Can I say hi to Tim?" Mr. Butler adds. "Hello, Mr. Johnson. I am looking forward to meeting you in person, but for now, this is mighty good. I like tree-climbers. I'm curious to know how big our tree is now. And how often you go to the park to climb those gorgeous, majestic oaks. There used to be a lot of them. My climbing days are over now, but not forgotten. I'd still say, after all these years, that my tree-climbing days hold some of the best memories of my life."

"Hi, Mr. Butler. It's such a pleasure and honor to meet and talk to you for the very first time. Your sardine can, note, and coin have changed a lot of lives here in Highlands. I hope you can come and see us. We can visit the old oak tree, too. I call him Mr. Green. I'm sure he'll remember you," I tell him.

Mr. Butler chuckles at that, as do many others on the call. But it's not an odd sentiment for tree climbers. Trees are our friends. They know us. They listen to us. They watch and wait for us. Johnny knows.

Our brief exchange moves everyone. The pause is palpable. It's not just about business. It's personal, too. This makes it worthwhile.

"I think one of the first things we might address on our agenda today is this matter of Mr. Butler's life story," Mr. Terry declares. "Have you written a memoir, Mr. Butler?"

We all notice Mr. Butler is shaking his head no, but Ms. Davis has their mic muted.

"I think we should share the list of questions that the boys and their parents have compiled with Ms. Davis and Mr. Butler. They can use that to stimulate his recollections of what he's done since he wrote his note and where he's been these past 50+ years.

They can jot down, at their own pace, perhaps by decades, chronologically, the highlights and challenges of his life," Mr. Terry suggests.

Ms. James offers to fax the list of questions to Ms. Davis, and also pass a copy along to Ms. Maples for her meeting notes.

"Have there been questions added to the list since I received the copy you gave me last Tuesday, Mrs. Johnson?" Sarah asked.

There weren't any additional questions, so Sarah committed to getting the copies sent to Jennifer and Ms. Maples.

"The next order of business might be to set a tentative date for a get-together at the Retreat to tape and interview Mr. Butler," Mr. Terry states. "Ms. Davis, what would you and Mr. Butler think is a reasonable amount of time to work on the milestones and highlights of his life, by decades, since we're trying to span multiple decades? Could you complete it in six days? One decade of history per day? And hopefully, address the boys' questions along the way," Mr. Terry notes.

Mr. Terry interjects a thought before Ms. Davis can reply. "It might even be an easier process if you recorded conversations with Mr. Butler for each decade, then sent them to Ms. Maples to transcribe. Or would that be more cumbersome?" he asks.

"Let me look at the list, and Johnny and I will discuss it. I'm confident we can get this done in the next five days. Don't you think so, Johnny?" Ms. Davis asks.

"We'll get it done. I can tell you that," Johnny promises.

"Simon, could your team go to Farland on Sunday afternoon? I'd love to do a meet and greet, do our interviews, tape some interactions, and see what we can piece together," Mr. Terry explains.

"Mrs. Johnson, would you and Tim be able to drive up for the afternoon?" He asks.

"I'm sure we can. It's just a 90-minute drive. Just let us know when to be there," Mom states.

"But I'm also thinking we won't be waiting until Sunday to visit with Mr. Butler. Timmy and Johnny need to galvanize their new relationship without media schedules and demands. It's not meant as a slight or personal attack. We just want some leisure time to get acquainted," Mom asserts.

"I appreciate your feelings, Mrs. Johnson," Jennifer says. "For me, it's all about getting personal. We pride ourselves on being family here. Come when you want. If you want to have dinner with us, just call ahead so we know you're coming," Ms. Davis adds.

"Thank you, ladies, for putting your foot down. I take no offense. We stick to business more than we should. In our business, we shouldn't need to be reminded that life is personal, too," Mr. Terry replies.

"Are there any additional questions, comments, or thoughts? If not, I'd say let's reconnect again on Friday morning to synchronize our plans for Sunday."

"Ms. Davis, if you hit any snag or want to float a question or comment, text or call, whichever is convenient. Ms. Maples may know more than I do most of the time, so reach out to her if you'd like."

"Well, it's almost 11 o'clock. I hope this has been helpful. It's been a pleasure seeing and hearing from each of you. Enjoy the rest of your day!"

***

"Mom. That was so lame! I'm so glad you spoke up."

"I think they mean well, Timmy. But they also have priorities to think about," Mom states.

"I'm thinking we should take a little field trip after school one day this week," Mom says. "I'd like to drive up to Farland and meet Johnny and Ms. Davis in person. Are you interested? What about tomorrow after school? Would you be up for that?

Just the two of us," Mom explains. "No newspaper reporters or cameras."

"Now you're talking, Mom," I tell her. "Call Ms. Davis and see if we can come for dinner and visit with them for a couple of hours."

"Who would want to wait until Sunday, anyway?" Mom adds.

"I say let's not wait -- to call Ms. Davis, I mean. Let's call her back right now. You can make it another FaceTime call," I suggest.

Hooey! This is so cool. Mom is on a tear. This story needs a major infusion of TLC -- tender loving care, as she would say. Would you put your parents or grandparents off for a week? Never.

"Hi, Ms. Davis. Timmy and I wanted to talk to you a little more. Do you have a couple of minutes?" she asks.

"You better believe I do. I'm so glad you spoke up on that call," Ms. Davis said. "I was wondering if anyone had remembered to bring their humanity with them to work today."

"Well, Timmy and I would like to come over tomorrow to have dinner with you all and spend some quality time with you and Mr. Butler. We really need to work on a closer, more personal relationship," Mom says.

"I would like to bring my stuff - pictures of Baker Park and our oak tree, and pics from the newspaper reporter that weren't in the article, my friends, their moms, the Treetop Gang. You know."

"And I want a new friend that knows a tree-climber's feelings. And he might like to have another tree-climber friend, too. I just wanted to share that," I tell her.

"You're so gracious, both of you, for calling back. The morning is finally looking like a bright, sunny day. Just call me if anything changes. We'll be expecting you and looking forward to a grand evening. Is it all right if I tell Johnny?" Jennifer asks.

"Absolutely. We want him to not only know that we care, but that his feelings matter," Mom shares. "See you tomorrow.

CHAPTER 15
The Shady Retreat

Wednesday Afternoon

Can you believe this, Timmy?" Mom asks. "We're about to shake hands with the man we didn't even know was alive a week ago. Is that crazy, or what?"

"I'm just so glad it's happening, Mom," I reply. "I almost wish Gramps and Memaw could be here to meet him," I exclaim.

"They'll meet him soon," Mom replies. "We'll just have to see how all of this unfolds as this week progresses."

***

The Shady Retreat assisted living home was a resort in name only. It was clean and well-maintained, but sparse in amenities. There were three separate wings of 12 apartment units each, arrayed around a hub, which housed the kitchen, housekeeping, common areas, office and work areas for staff, and medical examination and treatment suites. Outside, it boasted a treed landscape with a paved walking path, multiple flower beds, a 3-acre duck pond, and plenty of benches and tables with canopies and chairs.

***

"Hello, Jennifer. I hope we didn't hold up your dinner routine," Mom declares as we step onto the covered entryway to the Retreat.

"Welcome. We're more flexible than you might imagine. Once I told everyone we had visitors coming today, you became the focus of attention, and not that oldest refrain ever: 'whats for dinner'? That's a refreshing turn of events," Ms. Davis remarks.

As we got to the main double-door entrance, Johnny was standing there waiting for us. "Hello, Mr. Butler," Mom declares. Talk about melting your heart. I'm sure Johnny and Timmy were both on their tiptoes in anticipation of finally meeting each other.

"Johnny, here's your newest friend, Tim. Tim, I'd like you to meet the oldest tree-climber we have here at Shady Retreat, Mr. Johnny Butler," Ms. Davis said, with as much drama and exuberance as you can imagine.

It was a quick, formal handshake by both of us, followed by a hug I couldn't hold back. I'm inclined to say Johnny felt it, too, because it lasted a good 10-15 seconds. There were tears of joy, too.

After formal introductions between Johnny and Mom, she hugged him, too. I think we cemented a family relationship in under two minutes. It went way beyond description. I'm so glad we had these first moments alone.

And, of course, Ms. Davis had a heart-wrenching episode watching this special, long-awaited meeting unfold. She brushed aside her own tears as she ushered us into the dining room to meet the other residents, all sitting at tables waiting for the guests to arrive.

Ms. Davis was the perfect master of ceremonies.

"Everyone, I'd like you to meet our guests for the evening, Johnny's friends, Mrs. Betty Johnson and her 12-year-old son, Timothy, the tree-climber."

"If you've read the newspaper or watched the evening news story about the people looking for Johnny, these are the two."

"Let's have a wonderful dinner, and we can visit with them afterward, if you want," Ms. Davis announces.

Dinner was full of non-stop small talk. What grade are you in? What school do you go to? How often do you climb trees? How long have you lived here? Do you miss climbing trees? What was the best tree you ever climbed?

After dinner, we sat in the parlor. Johnny and I sat on the couch. Mom and Ms. Davis sat in high-back chairs across from us. I took out the coin, sardine can, and Johnny's old note first. He looked them over, front and back, top to bottom, and told me it was his dad who ate sardines. He said that the old oak tree was his favorite in Baker Park, mostly because it was so far in the back and seemed the loneliest. Boy, did those sentiments ring true for me, too. I even told him I felt the same way.

Next, I opened my cellphone photo folder and showed him pictures I'd taken at Baker Park after Mom said we'd be coming up here. I made it like a tour book. The first shot was at the entrance, followed by the field with playground equipment, benches, and picnic tables, and then a distant shot of the isolated trees in the back.

Then I showed him a great photo of Mr. Green, our favorite old oak tree. Finally, the best for last, I shared pics I'd taken from in the tree looking towards the sky, out across a few limbs, looking towards the ground along the trunk, then a video clip of 3-4 squirrels foraging and scampering across the grass. And I even had one of me looking up into the tree from the ground.

He said little. I wanted to think he was feeling transported back in time to fifty years ago. A minute later, he gave me a hug and kissed the top of my head. It was all the validation I could ever want.

Before we left, I gave him prints of the pics the newspaper didn't use for their story -- the Treetop guys with their mothers, and close-up pics of the coin and his note.

"Ms. Davis, if you want, I can send you the pics I shared from my phone at Baker Park. I didn't know if Johnny has a cellphone, but it's a handy photo album and easier to keep up with," I offered.

"Do you have a cellphone, Johnny?" I asked.

"I'm sorry to say, I don't. Seeing you with all those pictures on yours makes me think it's mighty handy, though. Maybe I should think about it," Johnny noted.

"I'd be glad to help you set it up and learn to use it. We could see each other every day, share stories, and plan things to do together," I told him. "You'll see. It's worth it, I promise."

Then, Mom chimed in, "Well guys, I hate to be the Debbie Downer here, but a little fella I drove up here with needs to get home and into bed, so he'll get up on time and be ready for the school bus."

"I know we've got a date for Sunday afternoon, so get ready, Johnny. We've had a terrific evening. I hope we didn't wear you out," Mom remarks.

Johnny and Ms. Davis stood up, helping ease us into this first goodbye. As we reached the door, I hugged Johnny again, thanking him for being my new best friend. Johnny kept one arm around my shoulder as he shook Mom's hand, then grabbed her wrist with both of his hands, clasping her hands as he looked her in the eyes and told her to bring this boy back soon.

Then, Johnny popped a surprise on us. "I know you've got to go, but would you be interested in seeing my apartment? It's just down the hall, and it won't take over five minutes of your time," he pleaded.

"We'd love to, Mr. Butler. Wouldn't we, Mom?" I chimed in. "And when you come to our house, I'm going to show you my room if you want to see it."

Johnny took my hand, and we walked side-by-side down the hall to his room. Mom and Ms. Davis trailed a few paces behind. It was spacious. The room had a divider coming off one wall that divided the space into a private bedroom next to the window on one side and a living area with a recliner, couch, end table, and floor lamp on the other. On the opposite wall was a 24-inch TV. Between apartments, a long wall contained the bathroom, closet, and dresser. Johnny had a picture of his late wife on the dresser, a Bible, and the newspaper article about our story.

"This is a picture of my wife, Eleanor. I called her Ellie. We were married for 35 years. They discovered she had pancreatic cancer, but it was already stage 4. She told me she didn't want to go through treatment that would ruin whatever time we still had left together. The doctors told her that was a valid concern and they'd respect her wishes. We had four more wonderful activity-filled months together before hospice came in to ease her pain and help her exit peacefully, which she did," Johnny shared.

Johnny wasn't sad. He just wanted us to know him better. How can you not love that about him, or anyone, for that matter? Life comes with some hard knocks. But we must get back up and keep on fighting.

"You're a good man, Johnny Butler," Mom said as she hugged him. "I'm so glad you shared your personal space and precious story with us. I hope when you visit us in Highlands sometime soon you can come over, have dinner, and share more about your life with Eleanor. My folks are eager to meet you, too. Boy, will that be a great evening," she added.

Johnny and I could have worked out a sleepover if it hadn't been a school night. It didn't pop out of either of our mouths, but it might happen, just not tonight.

Johnny and Ms. Davis walked us to the door. We all hugged one another one last time. They wished us a safe trip, and we wished them a pleasant night's rest. And I told Johnny to call me, just not when I'm at school. We both chuckled and parted, sharing light shoulder punches and grins, and I held my cell phone aloft, reminding him of how close we are -- just a call away.

I cannot explain what this evening meant to me. I could try, but I'd be sobbing. That might sound corny, but when you're having the best time ever, you never want it to end. Mom could sense that. She hurt, too. She's the best for making this happen and for everything else she does!

***

Sunday Afternoon

Shady Retreat, Farland, N.H.

Dad drove Mom, me, and two of my friends to Farland the minute church let out. The trip was quick. I guess Sunday traffic is lighter than on other days. We got to Farland well before our expected arrival time.

We stopped at a fast-food burger joint and had a fantastic meal. It was a mom-and-pop business, but it must have been a popular hangout for the locals because it was busy like there was no tomorrow.

Which friends did I bring? Even Mom couldn't believe who I invited. I invited Ted and Sandy. And there is a particular reason for each of them. Ted is the friend that sticks closer than a brother. It's inherent to him. It's the right thing to do. He's always truthful and kind-hearted. As a peer, he's my go-to for the straight answer with no sugar-coating.

Sandy is a bold young lady, outgoing, and a straight shooter, as well. I have a crush on her, which is true, but it goes so far beyond that. I'm eager to learn more about her. She's engaging, thoughtful, and considerate. I want her to meet and know Johnny as my friend, not just as the source and basis of a story. And I wanted Johnny to meet this girl who's become interested in tree climbing. He's never mentioned tree-climbing girls, but I have a feeling he will encourage her in her tree climbing for the benefits we see in it - freeing our minds to meditate, commune, relax, contemplate, and marvel.

All the groups agreed to meet at Shady Retreat at 3:30, but we arrive at 2:15. I can introduce Ted and Sandy to Ms. Davis and Johnny before the media takes over to do their thing. That's not by coincidence.

Jennifer meets us as we get to the door. "Hi, everyone. Welcome to the Retreat. It's so nice to see you again."

"I see some unfamiliar faces. Who have you brought with you, Tim?"

"Ms. Davis, these are two of my friends. We go to school and church together and like tree-climbing. This is Sandy and Ted," I explain. "Ms. Davis is the senior living coordinator here at Shady Retreat," I explain to them.

"I'm happy to meet you both. Just treat everyone here like they're your family. Most are quiet, but they'll warm up to you and talk your ears off if you give them some attention. Just pretend they are extra grandparents," Jennifer explains.

"I think Johnny is out in the garden getting some sun and exercise. Make yourselves at home. You're welcome to go out and let him know you're here," she adds.

Ted, Sandy and I race out the side door that leads to the garden, benches, and pond. It takes 3-4 minutes to find Johnny. He's about a hundred yards down the winding walk path on a bench with his back to the Retreat, busy feeding ducks and geese. It's noisy and wild. Every bird thinks Johnny's there just to feed 'them.' There's a rowdy cacophony of squawking, a melee of crazy, furious birds, all trying to chase away the others, running, pecking and flapping.

"Hey, Mr. Johnny. I'm back. And I've brought some friends who are eager to meet you," I exclaim.

Johnny closes his bag of seeds, grabs his cane, stands, and turns to meet us. "Well, hello. I'm glad you're here, Tim. Tell me who you've brought with you. I'm always hoping to make new friends," Johnny quips.

"This is Sandy and Ted, Mr. Butler. We go to school together and climb the oak trees in Baker Park, just like you used to do. I wanted them to meet you and hear some of your stories in person. And you'll enjoy getting to know them, too," I interject.

"All right, then. No more formalities. I'm happy to meet you both. I hope I don't disappoint you. This Johnny Butler secret treasure story is overblown, at least from my way of thinking. I'm grateful Tim found my note and coin, but my life is so much bigger than that little story. I want to live it up and mingle with real tree-climbers again who understand the importance of our treetop sanctuaries. Let's head back inside. It'll be easier to chat amongst ourselves in the parlor. These ducks and geese won't leave us alone until we do."

"I've got a surprise for you, Tim," Johnny tells me. Beaming, he reaches into his pocket and pulls out a new cellphone. "Tim, the first thing I want you to do is put your phone number in there. And your mom's, too."

"Oh, my gosh! This is so cool. I've got to put your number in my phone too, so I can send you the pictures I showed you on Wednesday," I tell him.

"Mr. Butler, I've only been tree-climbing once when Tim taught me how I should do it safely last Saturday morning. The world, viewed from a squirrel's perspective, was amazing. It was exciting watching the birds up close as they landed on branches, hopped around, and flew off without crashing into the leaves and limbs around them. It's a whole new, exhilarating dimension of observation," Sandy exclaimed.

Her comments touched Johnny. He reached over and touched her shoulder. Their eyes met, and Johnny winked at her. Connection made.

***

Sarah and Ben, from the Highlands Herald, got to Shady Retreat early, as well. They arrived at 3:10 and were raring to go. Their plan was to get in and out a few steps ahead of the TV station crew, if possible. Less commotion and certainly less congestion and potential for mayhem.

Ms. Davis greeted them as they entered through the main entrance double doors. "Hello. I'm Jennifer Davis, the senior living coordinator. You're Ms. Sarah James. I recognize you from the call on Tuesday. It's a pleasure meeting you."

"Hello," Ms. Davis. "It's a pleasure meeting you as well. I'd like you to meet Ben. He's our photographer and audio tech. He does all the heavy lifting in our crew."

"It's nice to meet you, Ben. I appreciate you both coming out on a Sunday afternoon. I know how hard it must be to get days off in your line of work," Ms. Davis replies.

"Johnny is in the parlor with Tim and two of his friends if you'd like to do your interview there. It's quiet and should be very conducive to your needs. Is that okay?" she asks as she leads them in that direction.

Ms. Davis picks up her portfolio of Johnny's recollections, beginning in 1968, from her desk as they pass by her office. It will help her remind Johnny of details during the interview if he hits a snag. She also gives a copy to Sarah to take with her if she needs it for reference when writing her article.

"Here we are. Sarah, Ben. I'd like to introduce you to Mr. Johnny Butler. Johnny, this is Ms. Sarah James and her coworker, Ben, from the newspaper, the Highlands Herald. They arrived early and wanted to get started, if that's all right with you," stated Ms. Davis.

"Hello, Sarah. Ben. It's a pleasure to make your acquaintance. I know you've met Tim before. These other adorable young people are two of Tim's good friends, Sandy and Ted," Johnny exclaimed.

"Mr. Butler, we appreciate you carving out some time for all of us to interview you and take pictures for our readers. It will take us about 30 minutes to ask a few questions, record your replies, and take two or three snapshots of you, Tim, and even his friends. Is that alright with you?" Sarah asks.

"Go right ahead. Whenever you're ready. We've just been chatting about tree climbing, getting old, making friends and enjoying life," Johnny notes.

The interview was quick and went smoothly. It focused on Johnny and me getting acquainted, discussing our first meeting and the future nature of our friendship. Ben took photos, as recommended by Sarah. A couple of minutes into the snapshots, Ms. Davis excused herself to meet the Channel 5 TV station crew, who had just arrived.

***

Mom and Dad met Ms. Arnold and her film crew at the door. Jennifer arrived a minute later from the parlor and introduced herself.

"Ms. Arnold. I'm Jennifer Davis. I've only heard your voice and seen you once over the phone until today. It's a pleasure to meet you. May I recommend a few suitable locations where you might set up and film? Please follow me."

They chose a quiet, bright corner cubby near the apex of two large floor-to-ceiling windows that had several lounge chairs and a sofa arranged for reading and relaxing. "This is one of my favorite spots at the Retreat. I hope this works well for you and the story receives positive feedback. Is there anything you need from me? Johnny is just finishing up with the newspaper crew in the parlor, so I'll get him and bring Tim along just as quickly as I can."

Sarah exited the parlor right at that very moment and walked over to greet Tonya. They had first met years ago and still cross paths, often covering public events and key news stories at the same time.

Johnny came out of the parlor while they were still talking and asked if he and Timmy could get a photo of all four of them to commemorate this news event. His thoughtfulness touched the ladies, not having considered the significance of the occasion from Johnny's perspective.

Ben quickly gathered the four, taking two photos; he then included Sandy and Ted in two more. He told Johnny and me to let Sarah or Tonya know how many copies they needed, and he'd get them out in the next couple of days.

Tonya told Tim and Mr. Butler to sit in the chairs and asked Sarah and Ted to sit at opposite ends of the sofa and listen with their hands folded in their laps. Ms. Davis sat between them. Tonya sat opposite all of us in a straight-backed chair and went over the planned sequence of questioning. She informed them the crew would shoot short segments, and she would repeat questions or retake some replies if anyone got flustered, frazzled, off track, couldn't think of what to say, or just needed a break.

The filming went well, and just like with the newspaper interview, the questions Tonya asked were like those Sarah wanted answered. There were several questions about Johnny's life from 1968 on, since TV viewers would not get their queries answered otherwise. Tonya wanted some outdoor clips of Johnny in the garden and on a bench for their lead-in to the monologue to the story, so the crew taped those pieces last.

***

Everything went so smoothly. My parents, Sandy, Ted, and I, sat with Johnny and his friends at a long table in the dining room for Sunday dinner, along with the other Retreat residents at adjacent and surrounding tables. We discussed the recently completed interviews, but mostly we asked Johnny about his time in the Army and his life afterward. This was the initial chance for any of us to hear about what he and Ms. Davis had put together over the last week regarding his life story.

Johnny was curious about Sandy's interest in tree climbing and whether she and her girlfriends liked it enough to try it again. He knew a little from what she shared earlier, but not as much as he wanted to know.

Sarah shocked Ted, me, and both of my parents as well when she told Johnny that she and her friends would indeed climb a few trees again if Johnny would commit to coming, watching, and joining in a massive picnic lunch with all of us and our families and friends afterwards.

Johnny, with no hesitation, committed immediately. "Just say when, Ms. Sandy. I love parks, trees, food and the company of good friends. Just tell me where to go and when to be there. Ms. Davis knows how to drive, and we'll be there to make it happen."

My guess is that Sandy has something more up her sleeve, and we might not hear the details for a day or so. She's a master at pulling off the unexpected. I can't wait to learn more.

Sandy was still in a chatty mood as we got in the car to head home.

"Thank you, Mr. & Mrs. Johnson, for bringing me to Farland to meet Mr. Butler. I know why Tim likes him now. I don't know if tree climbing makes old people feel young, but he is fun to be around. He's a good listener, and he understands us," Sandy professed.

"I don't have any brothers or sisters, so I've taken it upon myself to dive into relationships and be sociable. Be happy and make other people happy. Some of that I've learned in Sunday School and children's church, but I think it's a perfect motto to live by. What's that Bible verse that says, 'treat others as you want to be treated?' That sums up my philosophy of life. And I'm sure I'm on the right track," Sandy asserts.

"We're so glad to hear it, Sandy. Many older adults wonder how much kids get out of Sunday School and church and how other kids who don't attend learn how to become caring people and good citizens. I know you're on the right path, Sandy," Mom confides. "You're a good friend to have.

CHAPTER 16
Mega Pow-Wow!

Monday Morning

I could smell the bacon cooking from my bedroom at the top of the stairs. There's nothing better in life than the smell of sizzling bacon cooking in a cast-iron skillet on the stove. Well, it might be better if we were cooking bacon over a campfire while sitting at the edge of a forest gazing across a breathtaking mountain lake. But hey, it's all about the bacon.

"Breakfast is ready, Tim," Mom exclaimed. "Come and get it."

We had a great evening yesterday, meeting Johnny for a second time at the Shady Retreat in Farland. He's still young at heart and loves to engage with everyone. And he was so thrilled to meet my friends who were tree climbers, too. I think their feelings about Johnny parallel mine. He listens, connects, and has a wicked sense of humor. Those are special people, and you never have enough of them in your life.

I finished eating, was out of my chair, and on my way in a flash.

"I love you, Mom. I'll see you after school," I say, bounding out the door to the school bus waiting at the curb.

"Have a wonderful day, Timmy. Tell Sandy and Ted I said hi," Mom yells from the doorway.

***

I could see Sandy standing next to my locker as I walked down the hallway from the bus riders' entrance. Sofie was standing behind her, talking to another of their friends. We still had 15 minutes left before the start of our first-period classes.

"Hi, Sandy," I tell her as my mind races over the possibilities of our budding relationship. "It's nice to see you. Hope you enjoyed the visit with Johnny yesterday."

"I did, Tim. Thanks for inviting me. That's why I wanted to talk to you this morning. Sort of," Sandy explained.

"I wanted to follow up with you on what I'd said to Johnny that caught everyone by surprise. What I said to him was spontaneous -- it just popped into my mind and out of my mouth. I'm usually not that way. I was sincere, though, and now I'd like your help in getting this Baker Park picnic put together if you will."

"I'd be happy to help. How about I join you for lunch? We can brainstorm then," I tell her.

"That would be great, Tim. I'd like for us to plan everything, but we'll need your mom's help to organize the adult elements, like reserving the pavilion, coordinating with Ms. Davis, and maybe even inviting the media friends we've met who might still have an interest in follow-on stories," Sandy said.

"We've only got a couple of minutes before class. Sorry to take up so much of your time this morning. See you at lunch, Tim."

"No problem, Sandy. You can take up all my morning free time every day. See you at lunch."

***

Nothing new showed up on the lunch line today. The menu featured a few staple options, like tasteless burgers and cheese pizza slices. I grabbed a slice of pizza and a bottle of water on my way through the line.

The girls were sitting in their usual spot at the corner of the table. There were six girls sitting together today, though. All seemed familiar, but I'd only ever spoken to Sandy, Sofie, and Bernie.

"Hey, Tim. Glad you can join us. Bernie and Sofie invited some of their friends to join us today. I hope you don't mind," Sandy said. "This is Carrie, Becca and Charlie. They said they've climbed trees before with their brothers and cousins but never saw a need to mention it before. Isn't that cool?" she asked.

"I'm very impressed, ladies. You now outnumber the Treetop Gang. This is shaping up to be a gigantic tree climbing party. I can't wait for us all to swoop down on the oaks at Baker Park," I exclaim. "Boy, is Johnny going to be so shocked."

"So, Sandy, let's hear what you're thinking of putting together for this grand Baker Park picnic," I remark.

"Well, I'm only thinking in pieces right now, and nothing is yet in any kind of sequence," Sandy begins. "I'd like to have a picnic under the pavilion that will accommodate about 100 people. With all of us, our families, the media folks, Johnny, and any of his friends, we should probably count on at least that many coming."

Sandy then explains that the little kids will have playground equipment to occupy their time, and families can bring lawn chairs, coolers, grills, and whatever else they want. Ms. Davis can drive a van down from Farland and bring Johnny and some of his friends. We could have someone set up a winch seat in the lower branches of 'Mr. Green' so that Johnny can get into the tree if he wants. (The media will eat that up.) The picnic will be a potluck. We can solicit donations to buy drinks, ice, cups, paper plates, plasticware and napkins. We can solicit sweets from bakeries for advertising. We can eat after our group finishes climbing and parents round up the kids on the playground. And after eating, we can do some recognition things, have Johnny share, and takes pics, if people want to.

Sandy talked constantly between bites. We all sat there mesmerized by the volume of things she was effortlessly spewing out. Finally, I jumped in with a bit of sobering reality.

"Sandy, our lunch period is almost over, but I'd like to add a bit to the conversation for you to consider and comment on," I state. "I like the whole concept. It's bold and ambitious. But it's bigger than preteens can pull off on our own, as you said," I explain.

"We'll need our parents to buy into our plan and agree to take on some major responsibilities. Do you get what I'm saying? Let me ask my mom about this. Or better yet, why don't you call or come over this evening, maybe with your mother, and we can do some of this brainstorming with them." I suggest.

"Thanks, Tim. I knew you'd see the need for adult help, too. And your mom was the first person who popped into my head. She's been in on every aspect of this Johnny Butler mystery from the beginning. Can you ask her when you get home this afternoon and call me? We can go from there," Sandy says, with some sense of accomplishment and finality.

"Ladies, I think we'd better plan on a tree-climbing date this Saturday. We can do some snacks, brainstorm, and catch up afterwards. Heck, it might even be a great surprise if we did a FaceTime call to Johnny from the park under his tree," I add.

You could sense the excitement spike and intensify as the sparks of imagination grow within us. I even threw out that it would be nice if we included the Treetop Gang boys at our lunch table soon, so they felt a part of this. (I wanted no hand in a repeat of them feeling excluded again.)

"Thanks for inviting me to your lunch table, Sandy. Ladies. It's a great feeling knowing you consider me worthy of inclusion. I hope our friendships grow from this moment on."

***

"Mom, I'm home," I exclaim as I blast through the front door, drop my book bag, and scamper to the kitchen.

"Hi, Timmy. I set out an egg salad sandwich and some chips for you. Just a little something before you tackle your homework. So, how was your day?" Mom asks.

"It's been super cool, all things considered. I've got to tell you about lunch, though. It was amazing," I profess.

"Sandy asked me to have lunch with her and her friends. I didn't know there would be more of them. There were six of them altogether. And she said they're all tree-climbers! Can you believe that?"

"Anyway, she wanted to talk with me about her tree climbing comment to Johnny; you know, telling him the girls would climb again if he came to watch. Well, she caught us off-guard with that, but she didn't mention it on our ride home, which I thought was very odd."

"Well, she wants to have a massive picnic on a Saturday at Baker Park with Johnny, his friends, Ms. Davis, all our friends and families, the media people, and on and on. I told her it was too big an undertaking for kids our age. She agreed and wanted to know if you would help us. I suggested we get together this evening after dinner and talk about it. So, what do you think, Mom?" I asked.

"Oh, My Goodness, Timmy. Sandy has caught fire. I'm sure it's doable, but it's not a one-person project, nor can it come together overnight. We certainly need to discuss this and start writing out a plan. I suspect it will take two weeks," Mom states. "We must plan this far enough in advance for everyone to schedule it and avoid or resolve any conflicts. Have Sandy or her mom call me. We'll set up a time."

"Thanks, Mom. Sandy likes you and knows you are the best choice for this. You've been the key person in all the Johnny Butler activities," I tell her. "I'll call Sandy right after my snack and before I start my homework."

"Hi, Sandy. I talked to my mom. She said you or your mom should call her to set up a time for us to meet and discuss our plans. Shortly after we've all eaten dinner," I add.

"That's great. I spoke to my mom, and she's willing to help. I'm going to see if the other girls' moms are available to assist. It might be tomorrow before they respond. I already told them I think your mom will be in charge," Sandy says.

"Here's my mom's number. It's (603) 247-9812. Call her. Hopefully, we'll see you in a couple of hours," I conclude. "Bye, Sandy, I'll see you later. I've got to knock out my homework before dinner."

"I'll call her right now," Sandy exclaims. "See you later, Tim."

***

I hear Mom's phone ring just a few seconds later. Sandy's jumping right on this.

"Hi. Mrs. Johnson? This is Sandy. I just talked to Tim about my tree climbing and picnic idea, and he said to call you. I've shared some of my ideas with my mom that I shared with Tim at lunch today, and she's willing to help. Do you want to speak to her? My mom's name is Tracy."

"Hi, Sandy. I appreciate your call. You're very sweet. Please put your mom on the phone and we'll set a time to get together. Nice speaking with you," Mom says.

"Hi. Tracy? This is Betty Johnson, Timmy's mom. How are you this afternoon?"

"Hi, Betty. We're doing fine. Is it okay if I call you by your first name?" Tracy asks.

"It's fine, Tracy. I've heard a bit about the kids' plans. They'll need help if this is going to work. Would you and Sandy like to come over for about an hour after dinner? We can't get it all hashed out in an hour, but I don't want to run into bedtimes, either. Would 7:00 work for you?" Mom asks.

"Seven o'clock will work for us. I apologize for the imposition. Sandy enjoyed coming over for the media taping, tree climbing lesson, and riding to Farland and meeting Mr. Butler. It has all made quite an impression on her. This may die down or burn out somewhere along the way, but for now, it's a civic opportunity we need to embrace," Tracy explains.

"I agree, Tracy. But once you meet Johnny Butler, you may see there's a new relationship worth cultivating. He's not your typical nursing home old man. He's charismatic, principled, humble and relevant. The kids relate to him," Mom explains. "You might just get hooked on him. He's a saint of sorts, Mom exclaims.

"See you and Sandy at 7:00; our address is 813 Douglas."

"Thanks for the invitation, Betty. I'd better get dinner going. We'll see you and Tim this evening. Have a great afternoon, Betty. Bye," Tracy replies.

***

"Hello. I'm Dan, Tim's dad. Betty said to be expecting you. Come in and have a seat. I'll let her know you're here."

It's a quick shuffle to the kitchen to deliver the message that guests are here. Sandy and her mom are just getting seated on the couch as Mom comes from the kitchen, dishtowel in hand.

"Welcome. I'm grateful you could come to our house. Let's sit at the kitchen table and talk. That way, I can take notes and have our thoughts all on paper," Mom said.

As Sandy, Tracy and Mom headed to the table, I joined them from my bedroom. I'd gone up to retrieve Johnny's note and coin so Sandy's mom could see them.

"Tracy, have you followed this story in the paper or through the TV feature of two Sundays ago?" Mom asked.

"Honestly, no, Betty. Sandy has given me the gist of it, but we don't take the Herald and seldom watch the news on Sundays. Sorry," Tracy explains.

"Well, you're in luck. I have the newspaper article I can share with you. It's a simple, short story. It's just a human-interest piece that was intriguing and mysterious. Johnny went off to Vietnam in 1968 and left a time capsule of sorts for an unknown tree-climbing friend. It remained undiscovered until Timmy found it over 50 years later. That led us to wanting to find this mysterious, lost-to-time teenager. Now that he's found, he's become a bit of a folk hero," Mom explains.

"Tim, show Tracy what was in the time capsule."

After the Johnny Butler artifacts 'show and tell,' we listen to Sandy describe her plans for a huge picnic event at Baker Park, a reunion, of sorts, for Johnny Butler, who hasn't seen the oak tree he hid his time capsule in, for over 50 years. In some respects, it brings him full circle to where this saga began. And we get to celebrate his homecoming to Highlands, where he lived and grew up.

There was a bit of discussion on how Sandy arrived at a picnic for 100 and how accurate that number might be. Then, there was more discussion on potluck, donations, pavilion, etc.

As 8 o'clock neared, Mom suggested we adjourn for the night and whittle away on this project some more tomorrow evening. Tracy, Sandy and I were all on board. Then Tracy offered to host dinner tomorrow night in hopes we might have more time to work on the details. Mom agreed, and Tracy said dinner would be at 5:30.

***

I hadn't been to Sandy's house, but it was just five blocks away and ten minutes from our house. Whoa!

Sandy answered the door. "Hello. Mom's finishing up in the kitchen. Come in and make yourselves comfortable."

Tracy heard us coming in, popped her head around the corner and told us dinner was ready if we wanted to sit down at the table, which we did. "Sandy is excited about sharing more of her picnic ideas, so I hope you're ready for this. But before we go there, let's enjoy our dinner. I hope you like it."

Dinner was fantastic and went smoothly. There was some small talk and a lot of discussion about the picnic, timing, coordination, recognition, making a list of potential donors to solicit for help, outreach to invitees, etcetera.

Sandy was still full of ideas, which she unloaded in a flurry. As she caught her breath, she listened to comments, all along reiterating how great this was going to be. I was more than satisfied being the spectator in the room.

Mom put the tasks in a logical sequence. She told us she'd call Ms. Davis first to pitch the idea and see if they could drive to Highlands for a Saturday homecoming picnic. Then she'd call Ms. James and Ms. Arnold, the newspaper writer and TV anchor, to see about additional coverage. Then, on the same day, she'd call and reserve the park's pavilion.

Then, Mom would work with Tracy for her help in soliciting donations from grocery stores, bakeries and soft drink distributors for contributions or donations, offering event recognition of their generosity. She also wanted to find a face painter and a clown who crafted balloons into shapes for the younger children, as well as an audiovisual crew that could stream live shots to a big screen inside the pavilion.

Mom also wanted to mic up Johnny Butler for a Q&A session under the pavilion but would need to search for rental microphones and speakers and determine if the cost was feasible. Her initial thought, because our church used them, was to ask the pastor for his suggestions and possible participation and help.

And then, one more thought crossed Mom's mind. What if we created a Civic Service Appreciation Award for the Highlands Herald and Channel 5 News staff?

The only thing Mom hasn't thought of is a DJ. And if she does, Lord, have mercy on us. What kind of music would they play?

CHAPTER 17
Welcome Home, Johnny!

Saturday Morning

Mom and Tracy scheduled the Welcome Home, Johnny! Picnic Extravaganza to begin at 10:00 A.M. We were (all) anxious and excited.

"This is the big day, Mom. I know you're ready. Are you a little anxious?" I ask. "I'm so glad this is finally happening. I can't wait to see how Johnny reacts."

"We've planned every detail. I expect it will all come together and go very well. I'm expecting everyone to have a wonderful day," Mom shares. "It's for Johnny, but we'll all get a lot out of it, too. Just don't over think it. Concentrate on having fun.

***

Set up at Baker Park, in and around the pavilion, began in earnest at 8:00 A.M. Twelve dads were already there and had set up grills for burgers, hot dogs, BBQ chicken, ribs, and pulled pork. I could survive on the smells alone.

Mom and Tracy worked the merchants in town like this was a Fourth of July celebration. One grocer donated 300 paper plates and napkins. Another donated 24 rolls of paper towels and plastic utensils. A third grocer donated drinking cups and ten gigantic bags of candy. The Coca Cola and Pepsi Cola distributors each donated 200 cans of assorted soft drinks, bagged ice and loaned half-barrel tubs to ice them in. The bakery donated ten dozen assorted cookies and ten dozen mini cupcakes. And Highlands' lone deli contributed four party-size veggie platters and two platters of cold cuts and cheese slices. It was already a royal feast before the potluck dishes started arriving.

Mom set up an easel to hold the huge 'Thank You, Contributors' appreciation poster she had made at the local print shop. It displayed logos of each establishment and, at the bottom, asked guests to express their gratitude by giving them their patronage.

Dad and Mom brought four cushioned lawn chairs and two chaise recliners so that Ms. Davis, Johnny, and his friends would have comfortable seating.

All the media staff, face painter, clown, and audiovisual support were there at 9:30. Mom gave everyone an info sheet detailing the activity sequence, locations, and times.

***

Ms. Davis also arrived at 9:30 with Johnny and his friends. He brought two of his friends/dinner partners along. We had met them on our trips to Shady Retreat and knew the bond they had with each other, so his picks were no big surprise. Bernie and Ed were like Johnny's big brothers.

***

Kids began assembling for the tree climbing at 9:45. Mom had cooked up a surprise format for our tree climbing.

There were 15 tree-climbers ranging in age from 9 to 14, which was far more than I'd expected. I'd figured the four Treetop Gang buds and Sandy with her five friends.

The others might have been cousins, siblings, or relatives of the support crews. But no matter. More is better.

Sandy brought her 14-year-old twin cousins, Allie and Toad. This was a surprise for more reasons than one.

"These are my cousins," Sandy said. "Allie and Toad are mute. They can't speak, so they sign, with each other, mostly. But their hearing is fine. They'll give you hand and facial gestures, and you'll see that they communicate very well that way. They're both excellent tree-climbers, too."

"Welcome. I'm so glad you came," I said.

Allie and Toad went through the group shaking hands, helping us get comfortable with this unfamiliar circumstance. There were head nods, pats on the back, name exchanges, high-fives, and thumbs up, acknowledging one other and building new bonds.

"So. Are you all ready to have some fun? Johnny wants to see a great show here today," I tell them.

Mom had a surprise for us all. She'd devised a lottery. Mom gave each kid a number on the back of their hand. She had a knitted snow beanie filled with ping-pong balls with corresponding numbers on them. And mom had picked out five adjacent trees, numbering them #1 through #5. All five trees would have three climbers in simultaneous action.

Johnny would pull three numbers for each tree. Climbers would climb their respective tree for 30 minutes, then come down for a second draw, and then again for the last draw. Three 30-minute sessions with random partners on different trees in each round. You could swap trees with someone once if you'd already climbed your previously assigned tree.

"What a cool twist! Thanks, Mom," I said.

"No cheating, Johnny Butler," Sandy shouted. "We've got our eyes on you. No favorites!"

"Just remember, little lady. I came out to see how you young women do. So be extra careful up there. I'd rather not have to climb that tree and rescue you," Johnny told them with an obvious childlike smirk.

We had brought along a nine-foot ladder in case Johnny wanted to climb, too, but he said he'd better play it safe since we had a big day planned. He and Bernie and Ed were content to sit, watch and chat, point and laugh, and ooh and ahh occasionally.

***

Mom circled back to the pavilion to check on Tracy, who oversaw the setup. Food was arriving, and all was going smoothly. Other mothers hovered along the buffet line and helped keep the various food items arrayed in a semblance of logical order.

The media were out and about, taking pictures and shooting footage of the tree climbing, playground activities, face painting, and balloon craft, sporadically having interview discussions with attendees. The A/V folks were streaming live shots back to the big screen in the pavilion so that everyone could enjoy all that was transpiring.

***

Between the first and second tree climbing sessions, I checked in with the girls. "Hey, ladies. Is anything different climbing today than it was the Saturday you climbed with me?" I asked.

"I'd say it's not as scary," Bernie offered.

"It's fun climbing with different people," Sofie exclaimed. "We all want to have fun individually, but fun as part of a group is much better."

Then Charlie chimed in, "This is so cool. I've never climbed with anybody outside of my family before. This is not your typical way of making friends."

After round three, everyone gathered in front of 'Mr. Green' with Johnny in the center of the back row for a commemorative group photo. We lined up in two rows of eight, with the front row kneeling, just like for a soccer team picture. That turned out to be a blast, too. A party mood filled the air; new bonds formed, and the exuberance was electric.

Johnny then shared a few comments with the ladies. "Sandy, I'm glad you enticed me to come watch you and your friends climb today. And thanks for bringing your cousins, too. It's amazing to see friendships emerge and blossom as we mingle and interact."

"I've got to say, you've all taken this seriously and seem to sense there's more to gain than the sheer fun of climbing. You climb into a new world up there. And you control what that world will be like for the next 30 minutes to an hour. Becca, Carrie, Sofie, Charlie, and all of you.

You've lit up my heart with your enthusiasm. I hope you'll stick with this a bit longer before you get too busy and just outgrow it. You'll make some wonderful memories up there, by yourself or with your friends," Johnny concluded, as he wiped his eyes.

The girls engulfed him with hugs, smiles, and friendly banter. What a tribute and inspiration they were to the occasion, the relationships, each other, and all of us.

***

As we headed back, the famished crowd was swarming around the pavilion's perimeter, waiting for the starter gun to go off. But Mom had other ideas.

Mom grabbed a microphone, got everyone's attention, and then asked them to bow their heads for a prayer of thanksgiving. Mr. Tanner, our youth pastor, thanked everyone for their support and said the blessing. Immediately afterward, Mom said she wanted to share some rules for the potluck picnic lunch.

"Honored guests will go through the food line first. Johnny, Jennifer and the Shady Retreat guests, then our media crews, the A/V team, entertainers, pastors, and their families," Mom said. "Use both sides of the table and keep it a one-way path until everyone has been through the line the first time.

Once they are in line, I'd like mothers, big sisters, and/or grandparents to prepare their plates and help their little ones. As that line dwindles down, everyone else can fall in line. Help yourselves to seconds, and when you're finished eating, please throw your trash in the barrel receptacles at the corners of the pavilion. Afterward, we have some announcements and a couple of special surprises in store."

The picnic was flawless. Mom said there were 140 people altogether, so the turnout was fantastic. And no one got hurt, which most parents would classify as a miracle.

Mom had reserved a long picnic table for tree-climbers and the Shady Retreat guests. It was so cool to be with our best friends so we could talk, joke, laugh, and enjoy the atmosphere of the festive occasion.

As adults started clearing things away, putting lids on bowls, and stowing away serving trays and utensils, Mom took the microphone again to harness the crowd.

"Everyone. Please stay seated. We have more," she exclaimed.

"Sarah and Tonya, could you please come up front for just a minute?" Mom asked. Bewildered, and spurred on by being singled out, they meekly and timidly complied.

"Ladies, we met you just one short month ago, thanks to Johnny Butler's mysterious tree surprise. You embraced that story and shared it with our regional communities, which created a much bigger groundswell of curiosity. Even though in most respects you might say you were just doing your jobs, we see it as being far more personal. You are both professionals, and your friendly demeanor touched our hearts. Therefore, we wanted to give you a personal thank you with these framed, custom-designed Civic Service Recognition Awards. We love you both. Thank you for all you do for our community, but more specifically, for reuniting us with Johnny Butler and drawing us together into a wider circle of friends. You are bigger than personalities now. You're *our* friends," Mom concluded.

"The next thing I planned isn't a surprise for Johnny Butler; it's for all of you, the tree-climbing friends and climbers-at-heart who wanted to find him and learn more about his life.

Johnny, please come up and sit here in front of us. This is your Highlands Homecoming, and as always, you're a welcome guest in our hearts and lives. We're so happy to have you back in Highlands," Mom exclaimed.

"Johnny has agreed to answer questions you might have about his life, but one at a time. He's very humble, but he understands you're curious and want to know more, and he's ready."

"We've got two microphones we'll be passing around so that everyone can hear your question and Johnny's responses. So, who would like to go first? Just raise your hand. We'll bring a microphone for you. Stand when you get it, ask your question, and then hand the microphone back so we can keep things rolling. You can sit once you've asked your question. If you've got more than one question, we'll come back to you. Just remember to raise your hand, just like in school."

Apparently, everyone had shed their inhibitions. With one microphone in the pavilion's front and the other at the rear, volunteers alternated in recognizing guests who wanted to share their questions with Johnny. No one kept a tally of the questions asked, but in the few brief lulls, Mom reeled off one of the boys' questions she'd written down over a month ago.

Guests wanted to take snapshots with Johnny on their cell phones at the end of the Q&A session. You could tell it was a truly heartwarming experience for him and the attendees. Johnny is humble, thinking he's just a very ordinary guy. He might be an ordinary guy out in the bigger world, but not in ours. He gave us all an added sense of purpose, cohesion, and inspiration.

We're not just living for today anymore. We're living for the possibilities that are all around us. I now see Johnny Butler in everyone I meet. Maybe ordinary, but all are special, with stories waiting to be told. No superheroes, just super friends, hoping to get a chance to wow you with caring and kindness.

I've learned to live beyond the borders of my shell. It's fine to be introspective, but forsake the shroud of being alone and lonely. You're hurting yourself and depriving others of the uniqueness God purposed for the world when you were born. You will change the world through the hearts you touch, so be gentle, kind, inquisitive, and engaged.

***

"Hey, Sandy. Would you like to meet me at Dairy Queen for shakes, like around 4 o'clock?" I ask. "We can share some fries, too!"

"What's taken you so long, Tim Johnson?" Sandy quipped. "I'll see you there!"

Buds

I climbed them all, big or small

It was my task, no matter what.

They stood there, ever tall and proud,

And like a mountain, beckoned me:

"Come hither, lad, and try me out.

Let's see just what we're made of."

Wind-rustled leaves, swaying branches,

Enormous trunks, unbounded reaches -

I climbed; I perched; I laid; I rested.

All day sometimes, I'd climb - imagine

World adventures that I was part of.

Never doubting I was lucky.

Life was good without a worry.

Trees are my friends, and we are buddies.

Older now, I see anew.

Yet friends I made still hold their ground.

Though some are gone, some still remain.

They speak to me as once they did.

They whisper tales of storms they weathered.

We relive times o'er countless years.

They share their shade. They watch and wait

For the boy that was to come and play.

Copyright © 2011, 2025 by

Jackie Lynn Healey

Come Climb with Me Characters

Chapter 1

Timmy - protagonist, Timothy Johnson, Highlands, N.H.

Mom - Mrs. Betty Johnson, Tim's mom

Mr. Green - old oak tree in Baker Park

Chapter 2

Johnny Butler - author of the mysterious note

Dad - Mr. Dan Johnson, Tim's dad

Chapter 3

Ted - Tim's friend (Treetop Gang)

Tommy - Tim's friend (Treetop Gang)

Sam - Tim's friend (Treetop Gang)

Chapter 4 - (No new characters)

Chapter 5

Casey - Ted's mom

Bonnie - Tommy's mom

Lisa - Sam's mom

Chapter 6

Mr. Robbie Taylor - Highlands Herald, archives data services department

Mr. Simon Baker - Highlands Herald, Editor-in-Chief

Chapter 7

Ms. Sheridan - Tim's first-period teacher

Mr. John Nyles - Highlands Herald, City Desk Editor

Ms. Sarah James - City Desk reporter/staff writer

Ben - Highlands Herald photographer

Chapter 8

Sandy - girl at school, Tim's got a crush on her

Bernie - girl at school, Sandy's friend

Sofie - girl at school, Sandy's friend

Chapter 9

Mr. Jordan - Principal

Chapter 10

Mr. Nichols - Channel 5 TV crew chief

Ms. Tonya Arnold - Channel 5 TV reporter

Chapter 11

Paula - girl at school, subject of gossip

Marcy - girl at school, subject of gossip

Josie - girl at school, subject of gossip

Chapter 12 - (No new characters)

Chapter 13

Ms. Jennifer Davis - Shady Retreat (senior living coordinator), Farland, N.H.

Mr. Abel Terry - Channel 5 TV, Program Director

Chapter 14

Ms. Maples - Mr. Terry's secretary

Chapter 15

Gramps - Tim's maternal grandfather

Memaw - Tim's maternal grandmother

Chapter 16

Carrie - Bernie's & Sofie's friend

Becca - Bernie's & Sofie's friend

Charlie - Bernie's & Sofie's friend

Chapter 17

Bernie - Johnny's friend from Shady Retreat

Ed - Johnny's friend from Shady Retreat

Allie - Sandy's 14-year-old cousin

Toad - Allie's twin brother

Mr. Tanner - Youth Pastor

About the Author

Jack earned a BS from Park University and an MS from Troy University. He served in the U.S. Air Force for 21 years, retiring in 1990. He was an adjunct history professor for ten years and worked for the federal government in Maryland, retiring in 2013. He currently lives near the Gulf of America in Alabama and enjoys woodworking, reading, writing, and traveling.

You can follow him at:

jackhealeyauthor.com

jackhealeyauthor1@hotmail.com